HOLLYWOOD STARLET

HOLLYWOOD STARLET

DON JAMES

CUTTING EDGE

ISBN-13: 978-1-970848-12-0

Published by
Cutting Edge Books
PO Box 8212
Calabasas, CA 91372
www.cuttingedgebooks.com

CHAPTER ONE

HER HOLLYWOOD NAME was Kima Shannon. Sam Berill, a press agent, selected the name one night in his place after a dinner and show.

He glanced at a newspaper front page with a story from Yakima, Washington, and another from Shannon, Ireland. He beheaded Yakima and took Shannon for what it was.

"Kima Shannon is your new name," he said. "There's no other Kima. Shannon smacks of pretty colleens. With your dark eyes, black hair and impudent nose it fits you. You're Irish if anyone asks."

"Kima sounds like a Japanese name," she said.

"All the more mystery. Maybe your mother was a beautiful Eurasian and your father was an Irish adventurer."

"Sam, they're Ukrainians on a Montana wheat ranch. One ocean removed from peasantry. I have the high, Slav cheekbones."

"And the good, full breasts of magnificent women close to the earth—the natural grace, fire and energy. A woman for loving and bearing kids. But a name like Mary Tcharek for show business? A name people can't pronounce? Baby, you have everything else. Body, build, bust beauty—but you need a name. Kima Shannon."

At twenty-two, after two years of a state college, some minor raves for work you'd done in little theater and summer stock, a few off-Broadway parts, some TV walk-ons and commercial spots, you were ready for suggestions that might bring you more than the tantalizing taste. It wasn't too late to change a name, nor too early.

"All right," she said.

Sam grinned and finished his drink. He looked toward his bedroom.

"How's about it?" he suggested, half-jesting.

"No, Sam," she smiled. She finished her drink and got up to leave.

"I didn't think so," he said. "But it doesn't hurt to try."

"A dinner, show and drinks don't buy quite that much with me, darling. Just my thanks. And for the name I'd rather pay you when I get a contract. In money, that is." She laughed and kissed his cheek.

He shrugged—a thin, young-old man who had been in Hollywood too long to more than hope for a big break, and too short a time to earn it through the intricate ascension that netted big clients.

"You don't have to go," he said.

"If I stay it'll become a wrestling match and I'm not in the mood."

"Don't you like me?"

"Of course I do, Sam. You're lovable—but predictable."

Thus she acquired her name—several months before she got the spot in a TV commercial that changed her life.

She met Tip Lancaster at a party. He was young, impressionable, and a good advertising man. After his apprenticeship on Madison Avenue his agency had sent him West to handle some accounts.

"Kima? That's quite a name," he said. He handed her a fresh drink. "Vodka with orange juice," he explained.

"I know. You don't like my name?"

The party milled and spun about them. "I like your name," he said. "Kima Shannon. TV? Pictures? What have you done?"

"Anything to pay the rent. Legitimate, that is. Some TV—bits, some stock and things."

He grinned. "Hollywood's great question: 'What have you done?'"

"It's important, I guess. Only when you haven't done anything you have trouble getting a chance to do anything."

"Ever work in TV commercials?"

"Yes."

"Maybe we can use you. Do you make the ad agencies?"

"Some. Those who want to see the talent."

"See us tomorrow, Kima Shannon."

"You mean it?"

"Here's my card. Ask for me and I'll take you to Pete Farnow. He's our creative genius. We're doing some situation spots for a face lotion and we need a girl like you."

Kima thanked him, and thought that she wouldn't mind if something came of this chance meeting. She liked Tip Lancaster, but he was there with a willowy blonde, and after a while she saw them leave.

She went to the agency in the morning. Tip greeted her warmly.

"I hoped you'd come," he said. "Sometimes party talk isn't taken too seriously. I meant it with you. Let's see Pete."

He took her into an office where a coatless, middle-aged man stared at her through heavy, black-rimmed glasses from behind a cluttered desk. He blinked solemnly and looked at Tip.

"Pete," Tip said, "this is Kima Shannon—the girl I told you about this morning." He turned to Kima: "Our brain, Pete Farnow."

Soberly Farnow acknowledged the introduction. Kima smiled and waited as Farnow looked her over with the property-assessing look she long ago had learned to expect from anyone who bought talent.

"What have you done?" he asked.

Kima and Tip exchanged a glance of amusement. The great Hollywood question! Kima recited a brief rundown of her experience.

Farnow took off his dark-rimmed glasses and cleaned them with a tissue. His eyes looked tired without their shields of glass. He put the glasses on again and nodded curtly.

"Monday morning. Ten o'clock," he said. He scribbled a studio address on a slip of paper for her.

"What shall I wear?" she asked.

"What you have on," Farnow decided, approving her smart frock.

"Thank you, Mr. Farnow."

Farnow blinked, smiled and turned his attention back to his desk. Tip led her down a hallway to the reception room.

"Thanks, Tip," she told him. "I really appreciate this."

"Lunch sometime? Or a dinner and show?"

She arched her eyebrows a little. "You seemed awfully busy last night. She's very pretty. I wouldn't want to—"

"Think nothing of it. I'm unfettered, unwed, uncommitted." He brought a notebook from a pocket. "Phone?"

She laughed and gave him the number.

He said, "I fly to New York tomorrow. I'll call when I get back—and good luck with the spots. I think Pete likes you."

"Thanks, Tip," she said again. He walked her to an elevator and kissed her lightly on the cheek as the doors opened for her.

She touched her cheek on the way down. He was nice, she thought. For whatever it meant, he was nice. And she had a job for Monday.

Farnow handed her a script for the spot.

"We've decided not to use your voice," he said. "We'll use the announcer's voice over, pitching that a woman goes for the man who uses this lotion. From you we need acting. You look into the camera—his eyes. You're in love. You do a bit of business with eyes and mouth while the announcer plugs the lotion. We come into a big close-up toward you, as if the man is about to kiss you. You shut your eyes. Your lips part. You want to be kissed. Got it?"

Kima smiled and nodded. He gave more directions for a spot than some directors gave for a major scene.

There was some fussing with lights. A tired-appearing cameraman stood by a camera and waited. A junior account executive from the agency joined Farnow and looked at Kima with a speculative eye. She smiled at him. His gaze dropped below her neck and returned to her eyes. He was impressed.

Farnow checked the script, grumbled and complained. The studio crew tried to please him. The cameraman lit a cigarette, obviously bored.

In a sound booth overlooking the studio a technician timed a tape. He snapped on an intercom into the studio.

"I checked it again, Mr. Farnow. She'll have seventeen seconds."

Farnow went to a studio mike. "You're sure? It seemed longer."

"You've got a lead-in, the product picture, the guy finishing shaving and slapping on lotion. Then dissolve to the girl and tag out with the product picture and—"

"I know, I know," Farnow said impatiently. He turned to Kima. "You have seventeen seconds. Let's try it."

They spent the better part of two hours filming the spot. Farnow was a perfectionist. Kima was tired by the time he was satisfied, but she felt that there had been some good takes.

The junior account executive tried to make a date with her. Farnow thanked her and said he'd keep her in mind for other spots. The cameraman came over to her as she was about to leave.

"Making the rounds?" he asked.

"Who isn't?" she smiled. He was past middle age and his tired appearance might come from illness, she thought. His eyes were very wise as if he had looked at thousands of men, women and situations through the lens of a camera.

"You were good," he said flatly.

"Thanks."

He shook his head impatiently. "I'm not making talk. I've spent most of my life in this town. MGM, Paramount, 20th Century, Warner's, United—you name it, I've been there. Now I'm here, and that's my story. But I know when a girl has something. You have. When they start running this spot I'm going to have a friend catch it. It could do you some good."

She looked at him curiously. "Well ... thanks. I mean—"

He held up a hand in a tired gesture and smiled. "Skip it. I'm just an old pro who doesn't like to see talent wasted. There's enough no-talent making it big without seeing real talent overlooked. If my friend likes you, he'll get your name and number from the studio here."

He turned and left her standing there, watching his slightly stooped body ambling toward a door. The studio manager came toward her.

"Nice job, Miss Shannon. Be sure you register with the girl at the reception desk. We may have something else for you."

"Thank you. Incidentally, who is your cameraman?"

"Solly Bian. An old pro. Used to be one of the best."

"Used to be?"

"Oh, he hasn't lost the skill. He's still terrific. But he got on the bottle and then had two coronaries. Has to keep his work cut to part time. No heavy drag. This job suits him. He makes a buck and we're lucky to have him."

"Then he really knows people in the industry?"

"Solly? He *is* part of the industry."

She left the studio and retrieved her battered Volkswagen from a parking lot. Buying the car had been a heavy expense, even at used-car prices, but she had quickly learned that a car was almost a necessity in the Los Angeles area.

When she had come to the city, she somehow had expected the motion picture colony to be centralized in Hollywood; visualizing the show-business Hollywood as a separate and distinct small city in itself.

After she had arrived, she discovered that the "Hollywood" of motion pictures is more an idea than a reality. The industry is scattered over a large segment of the sprawling Los Angeles area.

She thought of her misconception now as she returned to her small Hollywood apartment from the Los Angeles city center area where she had filmed the spot; as she took the Melrose turn-off from the Hollywood Freeway, going north, past the Paramount studio's gates, the turn right at Gower, past the Desilu studio, Hollywood Cemetery, the Columbia studio. She might turn left at Sunset, glancing at Columbia Square on the right with the CBS modernistic studios. At Sunset and Vine was NBC's radio city, and to the left was MBC. Right into Vine and ABC was on the left.

Around the corner to the left was the center of the world for the people of two screens—the video and the movie—Hollywood at Vine, where Capitol Records' round building reminds people of a rising tower of platters and music from thousands of juke boxes.

She first had seen the corner at night in its full splendor of lights. Chet Gilthrem, a young writer she had met in school, who now was doing TV scripts, had taken her for a drive the second night after her arrival. Later she remembered the conversation and the evening; almost as if she had read for a play and the lines stayed with her.

"Do you like it?" Gilthrem asked, intensely, expectantly.

"Yes! Oh, yes! Because it's what it *is!* A sort of *symbol.*"

"I know. Exactly. I felt that way. I saw it and wanted to be part of it. I saw all the things a man could do. The plays I could write. The urge to write them. I was suddenly and deeply excited. It was almost sexual. I wanted a woman. I wanted to rejoice. I wanted to take, and have, and love, and create. This is crazy?"

"No, Chet. Not crazy. It's like that."

"Warmth in the groin! Swelling in the heart! Excitement! All the things to *do, see* and *have;* the people to *love,* words to *say,* power to *acquire.* God, it's wonderful to be young!"

She felt the contagion of his excitement. She understood what he meant; the almost sexual feeling. She felt it rising within her. This was the symbolic center of her universe. This was the place where she wanted to stand and greet and receive the world.

She remembered what she had read about the temple girls who in ancient times had prostituted themselves in the temples of their faith. Now she could understand it. Sex and worship may not be uncommon mates.

Later they went to his apartment where he wanted to make love and might have been successful if his own excitement had not betrayed him, much to his chagrin.

Her own awakened desire died with his failure. It never was to be rekindled for him with her; even as her first sight of the famous corner flared into heights for only one brief span of time on that night.

After that it simply was a corner—Hollywood at Vine—as it was to thousands: a busy, traffic-laden corner; a corner that she passed or avoided on her bread-and-butter excursions to the far-flung "Hollywood" workshops—Warner's in Burbank, Republic in Studio City, Metro in Culver City, 20th Century in Beverly Hills.

The necessity of learning her way around geographically was a problem in itself. Heavy traffic frightened her. She worried constantly about proper lanes of travel, turn-offs and directions.

Eventually she developed travel patterns. She became familiar with the well-known thoroughfares: Hollywood, Sunset, Santa Monica, Melrose, Beverly, Wilshire, the freeways.

As she met and associated with others the travel patterns broadened. She became familiar with the view of lights stretched out below Mulholland Drive. She went to parties in Van Nuys, the San Fernando Valley, and she knew where the bad fires had been. She discovered Malibu Beach. She learned where the beatniks hung out; the night spots; the expensive and the inexpensive; where to find name singers or bearded poets and bongo drums; the dinner-jacketed and evening-gowned, or jeans-and-sweat-shirts, skin-tight Capris and sweaters. She became familiar with the sweet-sour odor of burning marijuana—"pot"—and the peat-smoke smell of good Scotch in a drink by a swimming pool.

She learned how casually some girls accepted a contraceptive diaphragm as customary party equipment, and she listened to discussions about the new contraceptive pills.

Other things that she already knew became even more valuable now as she sought her place in "Hollywood." She could talk about The Method and Stanislavski. She became familiar with ideas, customs, traditions and some of the fallacies.

All these things became part of her before she made the television spot and a cameraman named Solly detected "something" in her work.

Within a couple of weeks the TV spots were running on local stations. Three weeks after Solly had filmed her, she received a call from Pat Sahnstein, who produced a TV series called *Johnny Methuselah*—a typical private-eye show featuring a smooth young star, Clint Clinton.

"Solly says I should look at you," Sahnstein told her. "I caught the spot last night."

"When do you want to look at me?" she asked boldly.

"Tomorrow at the PAK studio where we shoot *Methuselah*," he said.

When she met him she saw a short, heavy man in his early fifties. What was left of his hair was gray. His eyes were shrewd.

"What have you done?" he asked.

She smiled, unable to forget Tip Lancaster's remark about the Hollywood question. She recited her experience while the producer listened without expression.

"Stand up. Walk around," he said. "The spot was all close-up. Let me see you."

She stood and consciously thrust out her breasts and walked about, remembering all that she had learned about displaying herself.

He nodded and touched a button. A young man came in. "Yes, sir?" he asked, speaking to Sahnstein, but looking at Kima.

"I want to hear her voice on tape. I know how she films. I want to hear how she sounds. Now."

The young man led her to a sound booth where she talked into a mike, reading from an old script that the young man handed her.

"You better sing something, too," the young man said.

"What?"

"Anything. Just to catch your range." He was busy at a panel with nobs, dials, a taping head and a reel of tape.

She remembered what she knew about working with a mike. *Not too loud*, she told herself. *Keep it even, just a little throaty, and enunciate.* She sang a verse and the chorus of *September Song*. The technician nodded his approval. He reversed the tape and played back the full audition through a speaker in the room.

Her voice sounded good, she thought. The song came across. She projected.

The young man picked up a telephone and dialed.

"Mr. Sahnstein, I've got the tape on that girl. You want to hear it now? I can pipe it into your office."

He hung up, plugged in connections, snapped keys and replayed the audition. The telephone rang and he answered it.

"Yes, sir," he said. "I'll bring her in."

He replaced the telephone and winked at Kima. "He likes your voice."

Sahnstein nodded for her to sit down. "Solly's right," he said. "It's a bit—hardly more than walk-ons—written into five of the stories. You'll do. You got an agent?"

She had one of sorts and named him.

"How'd you find *him?*" Sahnstein asked, obviously unimpressed.

She shrugged. Someone had mentioned him. He was small and would take anyone and he probably wasn't much good, she thought.

"I could change," she said.

"It's none of my business," Sahnstein said. "Solly suggested this. You and Solly…?" He looked at her questioningly.

"No. I just met him that once at the studio."

"Didn't think so. He's sick. But you need a good agent."

"Would you recommend one?"

He shook his head. "I should be putting my neck out? I'll name three. Maybe you could think them over."

"All right."

"Milo Ginz, Carrol Laidenberg, Marc—"

"The first. Milo Ginz. Do you think he'd be interested?"

"I'll call him."

"Thank you, Mr. Sahnstein."

He reached for a telephone. "Thank Solly," he grunted. Into the telephone he said to an office girl, "Get me Milo Ginz."

CHAPTER TWO

O UTSIDE the Pacific surf pounded out its lulling roar in the warm night. There were no lights in the house where Clint Clinton lived except for glowing cigarette tips where Clint and Kima sprawled on a sofa facing a picture window and enjoyed the moonlit ocean view.

They had just come from a carefully planned round of night spots where studio publicity men had arranged coverage of another "studio date."

All this had come about because PAK—which was financially involved in *Methuselah*, and which had Clint Clinton under contract, being seasoned in the TV series—had agreed with Solly Bian and Pat Sahnstein about Kima. She had something. She had projected in her first part in *Methuselah* and she was being written into the remainder of the series. Through her new agent, Milo Ginz, she had signed with PAK.

Now the build-up was in progress. Publicity departments in Hollywood always have relied heavily upon fan magazines to help build stars. The magazines need news, and the PAK publicity department decided that a romance between Clint and the new girl on his show, Kima Shannon, would serve two purposes: build Kima and add to publicity on Clint. Studio heads agreed.

The couple was seen and photographed at Romanoff's, Scandia, La Rue, Chasen's; at parties and premieres; enjoying folk singers at the Ash Grove and small revues at Cabaret Concertheatre.

Fan magazines began to call them the new "Hollywood Ideal Romance." Layouts were made, stories concocted. And columnists began tagging Kima as "Starlet Kima Shannon."

Meanwhile, what had started as part of the job for Kima and Clint developed into a close friendship—although it was far from being the "torrid romance" that the fan magazines called it.

Usually when the rounds had been made for an evening—the columnists and photographers satisfied—Clint delivered Kima to the new apartment she had rented, said good night at the door, and left.

The magazine and column readers didn't know much about the getting up at five o'clock in the morning for an early call; the long, weary hours of shooting, the rehearsals, the takes, the strain, worry and hard work.

This night had been different. For one thing, it was Saturday night and no work the next day. After their last scheduled stop he had asked her if she would like to see his beach house, which she never had visited. It sounded like a good idea on a warm, moonlit night with no early call in the morning.

So here they were on a sofa, smoking, and watching the breakers curl in luminescent whiteness along the shore below them. They had been quiet for many moments, relaxed and contented.

Abruptly Kima said, "I don't know much about you."

"What's to know?" Clint grinned. "I'm too young for much to have happened to me. I photograph older and get away with the Johnny Methuselah bit, but I'm young. You know how young?"

"Twenty-one?"

"Twenty. I said I look older."

"You're always in a hurry like in *What Makes Sammy Run?*"

"I read that. But not until lately. I never did read much. Enough to get by a year in college. Maybe I'll go back sometime."

"If you didn't read, what did you do?"

He shrugged. "I dig cars. Drag races. All of it. My old man runs a small dealership. He wanted me to go into the business."

"You didn't like it that well?"

"I didn't know what I liked—what I wanted to do. I didn't like home, nor the town. Everything seemed to bug me."

"Did you do any acting then?"

"High school senior play. For kicks."

"Didn't you have a girl?"

"She played opposite me in the high school play. She got married that summer when I left."

"Where did you go, Clint?"

"I joined a magazine crew. You know? The old pitch? Like I was out to earn points for a scholarship and all that jazz. I was pretty good at it."

"And that's what started you running?"

He laughed. "You won't believe this," he said. "That was part of the training from this crew captain. 'Think positive!' he'd yak. 'Never let up—*think positive!*' And he made us run. Between houses we ran. In a room where several women listened to your pitch and one across the room asked to see your magazine list, you ran across the room. You *ran* and you thought *positive.*"

"And it worked?"

"Like crazy! And I guess I got the habit. Think positive—and keep running."

"That's how you got your break in pictures?"

"We hit a small Oregon town where they were filming for a TV series. They needed extras. All of the crew made it, and I got a break—one line. There was a girl in the series. We got talking one night in the hotel cocktail lounge, and … well, like suddenly I've got it made. You know? We went up to her room. The next day she talked to the producer and I got another walk-on and—what the hell, how does it happen these days? Like crazy. So here we are in my own house on a California beach."

He paused thoughtfully and then repeated: *"Like I've got it made.* An agent. A business manager to handle the loot they pay me. A press agent. Twenty-seven suits. A hot car. So I've got it made—and I'm not old enough to vote!"

Kima shook her head and laughed. "It's crazy, Clint. Truly!"

Clint turned so that he could look down at her. He was tall, broad and well proportioned. His dark hair was cut very short. His eyes were as dark as Kima's. His hands were large and capable, as if he might have been a football end or a baseball player.

Now one of his large hands deliberately cupped her left breast and gently squeezed. She caught her breath and looked into his face. This was the first pass he ever had made. She wasn't certain how it might be for them after this. Should she stop it now? She had better stop it while she still could.

"Why?" she asked, indicating his hand with a glance.

"I thought maybe we could make it."

"Did I make you think that?"

"No. Except, maybe ... well, most do, don't they? I haven't met many lately who wouldn't."

She smiled. "How about your girl in the high school play?"

"I made out," he smiled. "It was *her* idea."

"I doubt that. Is every girl a pushover for you, Clint?"

"Oh, for Christ's sake, Kima!" he said impatiently. "You know how it is. A man wants to make out if he can, and most try. You've been around show business long enough. You're no square."

"Does being around show business mean that anyone can make out with me?" she asked. She felt the weight and strength of his hand with a pleasantness that she was urged to enjoy a few moments longer. Only she had to let him know that she was no pushover—for him or anyone.

He said, "Because a girl is in show business doesn't mean that anyone can make out with her. Even in Hollywood where show business is something besides show business. Like … well, the chicks who come out here with stars in their eyes and no talent.

"They've maybe heard about casting couches and they start looking for them as soon as they hit town. Each one thinks she's got something special under her pants—when she hasn't. But she'll try to buy her ticket to all the goodies by taking off those pants and offering what she has. That's the way she thinks it's done."

"I'm not sure I like your ideas. Maybe you think I'm that way."

"No. You're serious about the business. You study and work and you've done all the right things. All you needed was a break."

"Maybe I did some of the other things, too," she smiled.

"I don't think so, but what if you did? What was I doing in that hotel room in a small Oregon town?"

"Whatever happened to her?"

He shook his head to her question and moved his hand to the other breast as he leaned down and kissed her behind an ear.

"She's going with girls this season," he grinned. "She's sort of 'ambisextrous,' as the saying goes."

Kima shuddered. She didn't like lesbians. There was something sordid about them. She shuddered, too, because his caressing hand was becoming effective. She placed a hand over his to stop the caress.

"No," she said.

"Yes. Let's make it."

"I don't want it to be this way with you, Clint. Let's not get carried away by our studio publicity and try to make it factual."

"I go for you, Kima. Like I *really* go for you."

He leaned over her. She felt his hands explore, and a knee pressed between her legs. She tried to push him away, but his weight and strength were too much. She relaxed and looked up into his eyes.

"No," she said again.

"The lady is a virgin?" he smiled.

"Just no," she said. His hands continued to explore. Her dress was going to be a mess, she thought.

"Listen, Clint … let's not? Please....?"

His mouth came over hers in a deep kiss. His hand achieved its goal and she tried to struggle away, but it was too late. He was awakening fires that she hadn't felt for so many, many months. Not since Jimmy. So long ago, and wanted so very much.

They were breathing heavily now and somehow they were off the sofa and on a soft rug before the picture window that looked out upon the ocean, too high for probing eyes on the beach.

He undressed her with a minimum of awkwardness as she lifted and turned to help him. Her breasts were free and bare to his lips. The naked, tanned skin of his muscled young chest was above her. She felt the hardness of his thigh muscles and the ripple of back muscles beneath the palms of her hands as she clung to him.

"So I have a low boiling point," she whispered. "So now you know, now you know...."

"We'll make out," he whispered. "You're beautiful. Here and here and here …" She shuddered again beneath his lips and touch and her thighs opened in invitation.

She remembered then. "Clint … use something. I didn't … I … I'm not ready. I mean—" At that second it was completely too late and she moaned and cried out as she clutched him to her.

"You'll make me pregnant … make me pregnant … make me pregnant," she moaned in cadence, almost in a plea rather than fear as the rhythm of their love-making climbed to a frenzy. She locked herself to him, and bit blindly at his shoulder, and scratched deeply into his back as she arched against him. Her low, keening moan of deliverance seemed to pulsate in time with the surge and roar of relentless breakers upon the unresisting shore.

After they had rested and were smoking cigarettes he said, in mock solemnity, "Now I hope that I do not have you with child."

"It isn't funny, Clint. I could be."

"Most girls seem to be prepared these days."

"Are you trying to blame *me*?" she snapped angrily. "I didn't anticipate anything like this."

"But you liked it."

"So?"

"Why are you sore at me?"

"I'm really angry with myself—not you. A man wants to make out, like you said. A girl—her reasons are different."

"I'm sorry I joked about it. I hope you're not pregnant."

"We'll have to wait before we know."

"Meanwhile, we can't do any more harm," he suggested.

"I suppose not."

He propped his head with one hand and arm and looked down at her in the moonlight. She shut her eyes and slowly exhaled cigarette smoke.

"Do you want me to tell you about you?" he asked.

"What's to tell?"

"Nudeness becomes you. Your breasts are full and firm and beautiful and you have rosebuds for nipples. Or is that too corny?"

"Corny, but nice. Also embarrassing to be inspected. Don't."

"But you're beautiful. The way your thighs taper in. Your long legs. Your shoulders. All of you. Let's make it again, Kima."

"Do you always get what you want, Clint?"

"It's positive thinking—and running fast so that you always have them a little off balance. We'll make it again now?"

"Not yet. No. Are you always so positive?"

"Sure. I'm positive I'll be a star. Shall I be positive about you? That you'll be a star?"

"Are you?"

"Maybe you're not going at it the right way."

"What way should I go?"

"Someone who is big enough to help you and who is interested enough. I don't have to name the case histories, do I?"

"Is that why you let me make out?"

"You know better. I've a low boiling point. You turned up the fire." She looked beyond him at the full moon through the window. "Tell me, Clint—is PAK a good place to be?"

"How many kids have walked off the job at PAK? Plenty. Including me last year. The only way I could get a decent contract. PAK stinks. If you've enough of a following—fans out there in front of the screens—maybe you can get away with a walk-off. No one likes to give up property. That's what we are. Property. You probably know."

"You think I'd do better if I slept with some fifty-year-old executive who could help?"

"You make it sound like a corny Hollywood novel. Casting couches and all. But frankly, yeah, it might help. You're good. Do you know how good you are in bed? All girls aren't."

"Short fuse, low boiling point."

"I think it's time we made out again."

"You didn't answer my question. Do you think I should go to bed with that fifty-year-old executive who could help?"

"It has to be more than going to bed with him. I mean, he has to be *interested*. Maybe you wouldn't have to sleep with him if you get him *interested*."

"Maybe you're right," she said. She dropped her arms and hands back over her head and let him bend over her with awakening kisses. "Do you know anyone like that?"

"He isn't fifty. He's about forty-two."

"Oh?"

"That's all," he grinned. "Right now *I'm* interested."

"I can see that," she smiled. "What's his name?"

"You don't know him. Not yet. His name is Ken Nytrack."

"I know who he is," she said softly. "Who doesn't? The man who made *Louie* and *Shadron's Dream* and *Corner Games!* Tell me more."

He lifted his lips from her long enough to say, "I know him. He wants to meet you."

"Me?" she asked. "But he and the great Marianne—isn't Marianne Thurlow his personal property as well as the star he created?"

"He still wants to meet you," Clint said.

She almost sat up, but his hand restrained her. "I shouldn't have told you," he smiled. "Look how much ground I just lost!"

Suddenly and impulsively she kissed him. "You're crazy," she said. "And now I know I'm not your girl or you wouldn't tell me about Ken Nytrack!"

"I would if I were just plain, ordinary pimping for you!" he leered.

"What a horrible thought!"

"But I'm not," he grinned. "I just like you. I like you a lot, Kima. I like to make it with you because you're you."

"That's the only reason I let you." She smiled secretly. "All right, Clint. As you said, we can't do any more harm...."

CHAPTER THREE

SOMETIMES when she should be sleeping, resting for a hard day of work, she tossed restlessly and tried to stop thinking about Jimmy.

It had lasted such a short time; such a brief span of days—hardly more than three months. This was during the year in New York while she had gone to the school of acting most famous for successful stars; during the time she had a small part in an off-Broadway play in which Jimmy—James Ogden Versal—gave such a fine performance and in which he truly crossed the threshold into the professional ranks.

Opportunities began to open for him. Television wanted him for some of the few live shows still coming out of New York—the big anthologies that could catapult a name into headlines overnight.

A Broadway producer became interested in him. Columnists spotted him: "Jimmy Versal … going places." The Hollywood fan magazines discussed Jimmy Versal: "the new, young, off-Broadway find …"

They met in the school before all this was to happen. They worked together and learned the fundamentals during the first few months. Jimmy knew more than she did. He had played amateur theatricals and had attended a university that had a good dramatics workshop.

At first they were just a newly acquainted couple; the black-haired, curvaceous young girl and the tall, blond young man with the clear blue eyes and the talent that was obvious even in his off-stage hours.

They had coffee after hours of work at the school. They ate in the cheap places, and eventually they went one night to his small, walk-up apartment. Somehow in their talk about plays, parts and people the talk turned to sex. Jimmy opened the subject, indirectly.

"You project," he said. "You *are* the part—the *woman*. You seem to *know*. Even sexually."

She shook her head. "Some parts—I don't know if I could truly do them. A tramp. Sadie Thompson in *Rain*— the others. I hate to admit this, I think—or maybe I should be proud to admit it. I'm a virgin."

He didn't appear to be surprised. "I know you are," he said.

"But in these days—well, even in my high school graduating class probably only a few of us were."

"But *you* would be," he said. "You're discriminating—certain."

They sat on the floor of his room. His battered portable phonograph was playing music turned very low because it was late. She wore a skirt and sweater. He was dressed in slacks and a T-shirt. Outside it was warm in late summer. She lay back on the floor, listening to the music, conscious of his eyes upon her.

"I love you," he said, his voice very low. "I truly love you."

"Yes, I know …"

"This talk about sex—I didn't bring it up because I wanted—I mean, it just happened to get started—"

"Because we're alone, and we're young, and you want me."

"Yes. You're more honest than I am."

She shook her head again. "More practical. Women are sometimes. That's why I told you that I'm a virgin."

"You didn't have to tell me. To warn me that I couldn't hope."

"I didn't tell you to warn you that way," she said. "Not to stop you." She smiled up at him. "I told you so that you'd know what to expect. If you want me, Jimmy, you can have me. I love you."

"Marry me."

"Perhaps ... later. We have our careers—so much to do first. But we needn't deny ourselves love. That's what I think, Jimmy. I really do."

"Are you sure?"

"Certain ... if you'll be careful. I don't want a baby ... and I may not be very good at first. Girls sometimes aren't, I've heard."

He looked at her for a long time. "I truly love you," he said again, his voice tender with feeling. "Only—only now I don't know—"

"I love you. You love me. Isn't that enough for now?"

He stood and turned toward the door.

"Where are you going?" she whispered.

"If you're certain, we will," he said. "But I don't want to get you pregnant. I have to go out. There's an all-night drugstore down the street. I'll be back in ten minutes."

"Would you like to have me waiting in bed for you?"

"Yes."

He was back in ten minutes, as he had promised. She waited for him in his bed, a single sheet over her nakedness, her heart beating wildly, excitement and anticipation already bringing hardness to the tips of her breasts.

She had turned out the light, nor did he snap it on. He spoke quietly when he came into the room. Enough light came through the window for her to see him clearly as he came in, as he turned off the phonograph and as he undressed.

"Are you ready?" she asked.

He laughed softly. "Yes, I'm ready. Just seeing you in my bed is enough. We're young, darling—so young and ready and needing."

"That sounds almost like a line from a play."

"I suppose so, but it's the truth." He stood with his back to her, and she could see his long length, the flatness of his back, the curve of buttocks, the sinewy length of thighs and calves.

He turned and after one, quick, inquisitive look she shut her eyes. She smiled and wondered if he could hear the pounding of her heart; if he could sense her fear, excitement and intense desire.

She felt him pull the sheet from her and the warm air of the room as it closed over her nakedness. She lay very quietly as for the first time a man looked at her nudity. She felt the rise of her breasts to him, the hardness of nipples, almost as if commanded by his eyes, and she felt the subconscious, modest effort to tighten the shadowed V where her thighs met, as if to protect herself from his look.

His weight was upon the bed and he rested beside her. She shuddered at the first contact of his body against hers, and then gasped as his lips found her breasts. It came very quickly after that. As he had said, they were young, ready and desperately in need.

She experienced pain and then intense pleasure. She felt a strange release and then a desperate, frenzied need to meet and receive and give and attain an undefined culmination that she sensed rather than knew. She screamed softly in her climax and he silenced her desperately with his demanding mouth as he crushed her to him.

Thus it began for them and it continued for almost three months; until the hour of nightmare that she would never forget.

It happened on a wind-swept, winter night as they were on the way to the more comfortable apartment that he had found. They had just finished the show and they walked in the cold with heads bent against the wind, anxious for the warmth of the waiting apartment and the bed.

As they stepped from a curb, a car swept around the corner. Somehow he pulled her back. She sprawled upon the cold sidewalk and heard the crash. She saw his body turn grotesquely in the air and thud to the street.

A taxi coming from the opposite direction skidded as the driver tried to stop. The taxi seemed to climb over Jimmy's body. The car that had hit him first skidded into a fire hydrant down the block.

She pushed herself up and stumbled to the huddled body on the pavement. The taxi driver was out of his car and kneeling beside the fallen man. He looked up as she knelt beside him.

"Jeez, lady … I couldn't help it! That car—"

"Jimmy … Jimmy …" she moaned. She looked into the face, and she knew He was dead. It couldn't be any other way. Death was in his relaxed features, his limpness, the stillness of his chest.

All the cast from the play went to the funeral. Jimmy's father came from a small town in Michigan. His mother was dead.

"He wrote me about you," the father told her. "He loved you."

They sat side by side in the funeral parlor, and stood by the grave. Afterward she went to the airport with him. He was a tall and somber man. Jimmy probably would have resembled him in later years. He kissed her on the forehead before he left her and pressed a card into her hand.

"My address. If you need anything. He loved you."

He turned and left her quickly, but not before she saw the tears slowly edging down his cheeks. She left the airport and went back to the apartment and began to pack.

She had just enough money to take her to Hollywood by air tourist and to keep her going for a month or so. Nothing was left for her in New York now. The big shows were becoming fewer with each new season. The off-Broadway shows offered something, but television was shifting to California. There was more work in Hollywood.

Besides, she couldn't stand New York now. Everywhere she went she would find memories of Jimmy.

She remembered all this the first night with Clint in his house above the beach. Until this night she had not been certain if she could give herself to any man but Jimmy and expect the deep fulfillment that she sought and needed. She had found it with Clint. Nor did she feel any disloyalty to Jimmy. She realized then that death had been decisive.

She and Clint spent most of the following day, Sunday, on the beach. They made love again in the afternoon, and he took her home early. They had a location call in the morning.

The next day on the set their relationship was completely normal. It surprised her a little. Whatever had happened Saturday night and Sunday had not changed their relationship in work.

Lately Sahnstein seemed to be taking an increased and worried interest in the series he was producing—to the point that he had taken on directing chores for some of the episodes. On this Monday morning, he was in the director's role and he was irritable.

The unit was working on a waterfront location. Much of the action centered about Carla Flaxon, a young and glamorous guest star who belonged, as Sam Berill, the press agent, put it, to the "sexpot school of acting."

The low neckline of her blouse revealed a firm, rounded bosom. Her blond hair was touched up to greater blondness. Her impudent nose, large blue eyes, full lips and richness of curves and hollows combined in a sexual impact that was wasted on few males.

She had appeared in three movies in supporting roles to upcoming young male stars, and she was a prime subject for fan magazine covers and stories that enthusiastically exploited her physical attributes, her way of life and her future.

At this moment she was industriously working on two jobs: to finish the episode of *Methuselah* in which she was appearing, and to make a conquest (not studio arranged) of Clint Clinton.

Sitting in the shade of a waterfront warehouse, Kima watched the techniques the blonde was using upon Clinton to suggest her availability. There was the breast brushed against his arm as they studied a script together, the hand upon an arm, the brush of a rounded hip against a masculine thigh.

The script called for a kiss between Clint and the girl. Kima noticed that Carla Flaxon put much more into it than an ordinary script would demand. She was certain that there was a subtle interplay of tongues, and just before they broke from the kiss—when the blonde knew that the camera had stopped—there was the insinuating upward pelvic thrust and invitation to Clint. Kima saw his eyes widen, and his smile as he looked down at Carla Flaxon.

Sahnstein had caught the interplay not indicated in the script and he frowned and peevishly snapped an order at an assistant director.

Sam Berill, who was handling what little publicity Kima could afford in addition to the studio publicity allotted to her, was sitting beside Kima.

"You're getting some competition, baby," he told her.

Kima smiled. "She's competing with the studio's publicity department—not me."

"Don't you go a little for Clint?"

"I like him, Sam. He's a nice guy. Just that. A nice guy."

"Carla wants to take him to bed."

"She has no great problem. He'll probably go."

Sam gave her a side glance. "Maybe so," he said. "She's the chick who's made casting couches popular again."

"Maybe that's her talent," Kima shrugged.

"Don't take her too lightly." Sam no longer was smiling. "She's a bitch. If she can knife you, she will. Watch her, Kima."

"What can she do to me? She isn't even under contract to PAK. She belongs to Gold Coast. And if Clint wants to bed her down, that's his business."

"She'll either be nice to you or she'll act like a first-class bitch. How has she treated you so far?"

"I'm not certain she knows I'm on the scene. Maybe she thinks I'm just along for the ride."

"Has she seen you work?"

"No."

"Let's see what happens then. You're good. She doesn't like other chicks who have talent. Either bed talent or screen talent, and you're screen talent, baby. What's your scene with Clint today?"

"They're setting up for it now. It's a sort of shaggy-dog switch to the plot. I'm the sometimes secretary in the private eye's office, as you know. I get clobbered in this one and Methuselah finds me knocked out. He makes sure I'm alive and in an impulsive moment he kisses me, and I come to. Just a nice, brotherly, employer-employee kiss."

"H-m-m. Well, make it good, baby. Little Carla will be watching."

Sahnstein was calling for the scene. Kima checked with a makeup man and she and Clint took their places. Sahnstein asked them to run through the action.

Stretched out on the rough dock planking, Kima shut her eyes and simulated unconsciousness. She felt Clint bend over her, the finger at her pulse. She heard his sigh of relief when—as the private eye—he found her alive. She felt his arm under her as he bent toward her.

Before he could stop the action without the kiss—as he usually did in rehearsal—she impulsively lifted her head and pressed her mouth against his, the tip of her tongue touching his lips. She felt his arms tighten and she opened her eyes and smiled as he pulled back. From the corner of an eye she saw that Carla was watching.

"Full of hell, aren't you!" Clint said softly.

"After Carla has you warmed up?"

"Nothing, baby. Believe me. Not with her."

"I don't believe you."

Sahnstein called for a take and this time Clint had to follow through with the kiss. He turned his head so that she knew their lips were screened from the camera and she opened her mouth and intensified the kiss even more than previously.

Sahnstein cut the action. "I don't want the kiss hidden. And Kima, stay limp. You're unconscious. Remember?"

"I'm sorry," Kima smiled. Carla was glaring at her, and Clint was wearing a small, amused smile. They went through the action again and Kima behaved. Sahnstein was satisfied.

"It's a take," he said.

The crew began to set up for another scene and Kima walked toward the chairs reserved for the cast. Carla looked at her.

"Just a studio romance between you two?" The blonde smiled.

"What do you mean?" Kima asked innocently.

"That kiss. It looked like you were rehearsing for the first night in a honeymoon."

Kima smiled and went by the girl and found a chair some distance away. She had drawn blood from the blonde starlet. Carla had left her chair and was talking with Clint, close to him, touching him.

Sam rejoined Kima. "She didn't like it," he observed. "She wants him."

"Obviously. Where is she from, Sam? I mean, really? Not that story the studio put out about her mother being a widow, her father a war hero, and Carla being just a winsome, homespun gal at heart."

Sam laughed. "A Gold Coast director saw her in a Vegas club. She was in one of the bare-breasted lines. Before that she worked cheap nighteries in Chicago. And before that she was shacking up with a crowd of juvenile delinquents. She's been around."

"In a very few years."

"It doesn't take long to learn what she does best."

"You're a bitter, cynical, shocking man, Sam," Kima smiled.

"Just realistic. Watch her, Kima. She doesn't like you."

"Sam, I couldn't care less."

Kima said the words in complete honesty. She didn't care what Carla thought or did. She wasn't worried about Clint and Carla, mainly because she realized that she was not in love with Clint. What had happened between them simply had happened. If there was any deep feeling toward him, it was in appreciation to him for finally delivering her from the inhibiting memories of Jimmy.

Her brief meditation was interrupted by angry words near a camera where Sahnstein had joined Clint and Carla Flaxon. Clint was glaring at the producer.

"You can go to hell!" he shouted. "You and PAK and the whole goddamn setup of creeps that you represent! I don't need you."

"By God you'll do the scene the way I tell you!" Sahnstein yelped, visibly trembling with anger. "Either that or—"

"Or what?" Clinton interrupted. He smiled at the producer with anything but humor—a mocking, defiant, disdainful smile.

Carla took the opportunity to crowd behind him so that her full-blown young body pressed close to him. She clutched at the bicep of his right arm as if to prevent him from striking Sahnstein.

Sahnstein took a deep, careful breath and sunk his hands into his pockets. Members of the crew watched with anticipation. An assistant director hovered near the group, trying to voice a conciliatory thought.

"You're under contract," Sahnstein said in slow, angry cadence. "And you can be suspended. Don't forget it, Clinton."

"Who'll do it? Not you, Sahnstein. I'm on loan to you. PAK holds my contract."

"Do you want to make a test case of it?"

"You wouldn't try," Clinton smiled. "You've got to finish the series. You've still got five to put in the can."

Carla tugged at Clinton's arm. "Honey, it isn't *worth* it! Of course he needs you! We all do! But it isn't worth getting upset about."

"The hell it isn't!" Clinton snapped.

"No, baby … please?" Carla moved against him. "For me? We'll do the scene and then we'll be through for the day, and we have tonight. Let's not spoil tonight, honey."

Clinton relaxed and patted the small, feminine hand on his arm.

"All right, baby. I guess you're right." He smiled the humorless smile at Sahnstein again. "Let's get it done. But the way you can louse up a scene, Sahnstein—you're a gasser. A real gasser!"

Sahnstein started to say something, then shrugged and turned to the assistant director. "You take it," he said. "It isn't important enough—any bit player could do it." He turned and stalked away.

Kima glanced at Sam. "That's interesting," she said. "The studio has us set for an appearance at the opening of that new supper club on the Strip tonight. I wonder if we take Carla along."

"I hope not," Sam said. "I don't want him screwing up your publicity. The boys at PAK won't like it either. I don't think they'll want him shacking up with that Carla dame. She doesn't help create the image of the all-American-type boy they're trying to make him into. A month with her and he'll be the exhausted-type ex-lover."

"Sam, I think you're envious!" Kima laughed.

"I wouldn't turn my back on her," he admitted. "But I'd sure as hell keep my eye on my wallet while the fun was going on."

"You're unkind."

"I told you. I'm realistic. Now, with you—"

"With me there isn't a chance. We decided that long ago."

"Yeah, I know," Sam said. He stood. "I have to go. I've other clients, even if I wish I didn't. I guess the boys from the studio will handle tonight. Or do you think I should be around—in view of lover boy's upcoming conflict date with glamour pants?"

"Don't worry about it. The studio people will be there."

Sam nodded in agreement and left, walking toward his three-year-old car. She watched him, realizing that she was genuinely fond of the thin, dissipated press agent. Somehow she knew that he was a friend in a place where friends were truly few and far between.

Kima took longer than usual preparing for the studio-inspired date that she was supposed to have with Clint Clinton. Now, after a long, lazy bath, she lay nude on her bed, relaxing, and staring at the ceiling as she thought about the day and the things that had happened.

Nothing had been too important. She had seen Carla Flaxon in action, and she was a little annoyed with the blonde's sudden conquest of Clinton, but she was not jealous. She had seen Clint lose his temper, and Pat Sahnstein was on edge about something. Otherwise the day hadn't amounted to much and she had no call for the morning—a day off.

The evening could be something else, though. She wondered what complications might be in store for her, and she was tempted to call Clint to find out about their date. Obviously he had some sort of a conflicting date with Carla Flaxon.

"Unless," she thought, "his date with her is after he leaves me."

That, obviously, might be a bedroom date and despite her lack of jealousy, and knowing that she did not love Clint Clinton, the idea nettled her. What could Carla Flaxon offer that she couldn't?

She glanced down at her nude body, the firm young breasts, the long legs, the soft, shadowy contours of her most vital femininity. Tentatively she cupped her breasts. She passed the palms of her hands down her flanks and along the inner smoothness of her thighs.

It was strange, she thought, how intimate a woman might be with her own body; caressing it with hands that abruptly were not her own hands, but a lover's hands. Thus she seemed to feel the texture of her skin, the body richness and firmness through strange hands. And in the exploration her body responded.

She thought how it had been so recently with Clint. A warm lassitude crept through her so that her caresses became more intimate, even with herself, and she allowed her body to move with the natural reflex movements that came from the gentle arousal.

She awoke with a start. Her telephone was ringing. Hurriedly she answered, glancing at a bedside clock. Actually she had slept only a few moments. She was not late.

"It's me, Chickie," Clint Clinton said. "About tonight. Mind if we make it a foursome?"

"Why should I mind?" she asked, shortly. She might have suspected that this would happen. "Why don't you ask the studio?"

"Don't be this way, baby. I've got a nice date for you. We're going to work it sort of diplomatic like. I'll take you to the joint—the other couple will join us there. All casual so the studio boys won't tumble. After we leave together, we're on our own."

"And who is this date who's going to be so nice for me?"

"Ken Nytrack," Clint said. "I told you he wants to meet you. I called him and he went for this idea."

The name came as a distinct surprise to Kima, and she felt a small tremor of excitement. She had long admired Ken Nytrack for his ability, his power and his independence in a world where independence actually was at a premium. When a man like Ken Nytrack backed a girl—

"You still there?" Clint asked.

Kima took a deep breath. "I'm here," she said. "All right, Clint. And—thanks. I mean, I really should thank you."

"I like you, baby. You know that. Like you for real. And I'm doing a favor for both of you."

"How about you?"

"Carla. Okay with you?"

"Of course. And after we leave that place?"

"Out to Nytrack's place in Beverly Hills."

They finished their conversation and Kima went into her bathroom. She needed to do a little with her hair, and makeup, and ...

She hesitated and thoughtfully looked into her own eyes in a mirror and asked herself an honest question. *How honest can you be with yourself?* she thought. *How much will you do for a career? How much do you value yourself and what you have? How practical will you be?*

Almost ruefully she smiled at her own image. "Be practical," she said.

She went to a chest of drawers and pulled one out. She searched to the bottom of it and found a small box.

When Jimmy had died, she had thought of throwing away the box and its contents. It seemed that she would never need them again. And now as she looked at the box she remembered the visit to the New York doctor, with her dime-store wedding band on a finger, and the rest of the lie: that she was a bride and understood that a certain method ...

"It's probably the best mechanical contraceptive means for a woman to use," the doctor said. "I'll be glad to fit you and instruct you."

Now she remembered the doctor's impersonal and careful instructions. She remembered, too, that she and Clint had fallen into the trap of a moonlit night only hours ago, and that she had been unprepared.

Whatever regrets she might have about that now, she did know that she could be awakened physically again, and that she could be defenseless.

She opened the box. She would be ready.

CHAPTER FOUR

THE NIGHT CLUB was new and expensive. Backed by enough money, friends and entertainment to assure a successful opening on a Monday night, it was one of the changing names and ownerships along Sunset Strip's famous stretch of glamour.

Kima knew some of the history of the strip and its plush bistros. She recognized the Crescendo. She knew where the site of Playboy's Key Club would be—where the Mocambo and the Cloister had been. She knew Le Crazy Horse that once had been Ciro's, and—of course—Cyrano's.

The new place was on an old site. The decor was fresh, the cuisine was exotic, the drinks were powerful, most of the faces were familiar, and the name attraction was fresh from Las Vegas, where his dry, sophisticated wisecracks had tabbed him as expensive talent.

When they arrived the new club was crowded. Photographers were busy. The opening was a success.

The studio had arranged a table for them. They had been seated a short time when Kima looked up into the eyes of Carla Flaxon. The blonde was smiling tightly, almost angrily. Kima wondered if Carla Flaxon might not wish that Ken Nytrack could have been her date for the night. Certainly Carla was willing to sell to the highest bidder, and Ken Nytrack could outbid Clint Clinton.

"He wants to meet *you*, dear," Carla emphasized, still wearing the tight smile. "Ken, this is Kima Shannon."

Kima already was looking into the level, pleasant eyes of the man who stood behind Carla. In that instant she realized that the pictures she had seen of Ken Nytrack had failed to capture the real man. Only in a live projection could anyone truly sense Nytrack's energy, confidence and vitality.

He smiled and spoke her name. Clint made a small business of greeting them, motioning for additional chairs, seating Carla.

Ken Nytrack remained standing, still looking down at Kima, smiling, saying nothing. Kima knew that her eyes were as unwavering as his, that she must appear to be transfixed by his gaze.

"Have they finished your publicity bit?" Nytrack said to Clint.

"I guess so. I saw Mike—he's a studio man—leave about ten minutes ago. I guess we're in the clear."

"Then let's go," Nytrack said. He turned his attention again to Kima. "Is that all right with you?"

"I have a choice?"

"I hope not!" he laughed. "But you know this was all arranged, so why play it any other way? You can ride with me."

"Where are we going?"

"My place."

Their eyes locked again. "I don't know," she said, hesitantly, almost in a whisper, and not knowing why she was hesitant. Clint already was on his feet and Carla was smiling her cat smile and getting up.

"That's better than here!" Carla said.

Outside Nytrack helped Kima into an expensive Italian sports car.

"You'll like my place," he said. "We'll meet Clint and Carla there."

"We're really going in for alliteration tonight," Kima said, thinking that her remark sounded inane. "All K sounds. Clint, Carla, Kima and Ken."

"Maybe that's significant."

"Just alliteration," she said and sat back in the luxury of a molded seat that seemed to wrap her in a reassuring embrace.

He drove skillfully and fast. Eventually he turned into a driveway that led through landscaped grounds to a mansion.

"It's old and rather famous," he said. "I like large things and seclusion. Two silent stars owned it."

He took her into the mansion to a wood-paneled room that was larger than most modern living rooms.

"They called this a den," he said. He crossed to a large hi-fi console, and music in stereo from a tape subtly filled the room. He moved to a small bar and indicated bottles.

"Will you drink Scotch with me?" he smiled.

"I like it."

"Good. Too many seem to prefer vodka these days."

"I know. The vodka and juice crowd. Actually, I *should* like it."

He looked a question at her.

"My folks are Russian," she explained. "Ukrainian."

"You'll still have Scotch?"

"Of course."

He nodded his satisfaction and brought the drinks with him. She watched him cross the room and he reminded her of the lean, hard-muscled, professional football quarterbacks she had seen; efficiently compact and dangerously quick. She wondered why she observed men in relation to athletics.

His hair was dark brown, gray-touched and cut close to his scalp. His mouth was firm and given to quick but thin smiles. She sensed that it could be an angry mouth, and that the pleasant voice could be cutting.

She felt a disturbing uneasiness. He did something to her. He created a strange, nameless restlessness in her. She wanted some undefined quality of manhood from him; more than his obvious physical qualities.

"He's a man," she thought. "He's a man, as Clint is a boy, as Jimmy was a boy. He doesn't have to experiment. He's certain. He knows. He knows exactly what to do with a woman, and a woman can't teach him anything—she can only receive and learn from him."

She realized that she never had thought of any other man in this way, and for a strange, unreal moment she had a tremendous urge to touch him, to press against him, to bestow her femininity upon him.

If he recognized what was happening to her, he hid the knowledge with his quiet smile. He took her to a leather-covered sofa. They sat and sipped at their drinks, their eyes meeting over the glasses.

"Tell me about yourself," he suggested.

"You mean, 'What have you done?' " she smiled.

He laughed. "I know what you've done. Studied in New York, appeared in an off-Broadway production. Some TV work, a damn good TV commercial for a face lotion, which, in turn, got you a spot with Pat Sahnstein, via an old-time cameraman, Solly Bian, who is my friend, too."

"You know quite a bit about me."

"I've seen you at Cyrano's, and in some other places on the Strip."

"I've never seen you there."

He shrugged. "I do most of my business in an office or here."

"You mean you don't approve of the Strip and the places on it?"

"Every industry seems to have a center of activity where the deals are made. Finance has Wall Street, the advertising people claim Madison Avenue. The garment business has its street, diamond merchants theirs—also there's Broadway and there's Forty-second Street. In the film industry it seems to be Sunset Boulevard—and the Strip. That means from Sweetzer Drive westward to the boundary of Beverly Hills, at Doheny Drive. Fifteen blocks—and just about everything that anyone could want, but mostly The Industry." He paused and smiled ruefully. "I didn't mean to lecture."

"It's not a lecture," she said. "And I know a little what you mean. I love it. I love to drink *capuccino* at Cyrano's or Chez Paulette, the Via Veneto. I like to watch the girls make their entrances in Capris and piled hair-dos and hopes! I love to listen to the talk—the writers, producers, directors, agents and all the kids like me trying to get somewhere, somehow. I like Cyrano's best."

He studied her intently, a quizzical expression on his face.

"I wonder if I'm getting old," he said. "Or tired. You know … the faces there today aren't the ones that were there two years ago. It changes fast. Everything changes fast. I'm forty-two, and sometimes I think I'm really too old for this business."

"That's foolish talk. You're not old. You're—I hate the phrase—'in the prime.' You're … *vital*."

He shook his head. "I think I'm seeing the last big changes, and I'm glad I was here before some of them happened. I mean back when the studio and star system was all-important."

"It's different now?"

He finished his drink and offered her a cigarette. She took one and he lit it and then got fresh drinks for them.

"It's different," he said flatly. "Television came—with some other things—and changed it. Do you know what's happening to the studios?"

"I've heard."

"Half the studios are used for television shows or commercials. Fox sold its big West Los Angeles lot for some forty million dollars and rents back seventy-five acres. What's going in? Two hundred acres of apartments! Look at the great sets that are gone—the fabulous sets they kept year after year. Even Fox's 'Tombstone Street.' The Warner ranch is a real estate development. That—skip it; it's part of progress."

"They're still making big pictures."

"Certainly. In Italy, England, Japan—out on location. International location, that is."

"That's bad?"

He shook his head in some sudden secret amusement. "I forget," he said. "You're one of the youngsters, too."

"Not that young," she said. "Perhaps in years—but I've read and I still can remember?"

"The big ones?" he asked. "Do you really remember Gable and Cooper, Garbo, the Barrymores, and—?"

"Certainly," she interrupted. "Don't forget we've all had a course in motion picture history through the late shows on TV."

"You mean you've studied them?"

"If we're at all serious about the business."

"Yes, I suppose you would—I mean *you*. You've worked at it."

"I know kids who can name complete casts of pictures filmed twenty years ago," she said. "I knew a boy named Jimmy Versal who—"

"You lived with him in New York. He was killed. He was good. He would have made it. I could have used him later."

She stared at him. "You pry," she said, defensive and angry.

"No. I'm interested in you. I wanted to know all there is to know about you. I checked. If you happened to live with him—" He shrugged. "You might have been secretly married—you might have preferred it that way. Don't make it difficult for us by being edgy."

"Just what do you want of me?"

"You know what I want of you. Or you should know. You're smart enough. I want to make something of you; to put you in a picture; build you into something far better than PAK could ever make of you with their chain line operation."

"That's all?"

"No," he said thoughtfully. "Not after this evening—just this short time. I also want you."

"I suppose it's corny to ask if this is the casting couch bit. But is it?"

"What do you think, Kima? You seem to know a little about me. You haven't heard my name linked very often with a woman's. I was married and divorced. Since then—nothing very serious. Just a normal man's way of living in this environment."

"That's what I mean. Am I just part of the normal environment?"

"No. I wouldn't be offering the rest if you were."

"Maybe this is just the package deal you're offering," she smiled. "Maybe you think you could really make something of me, so you'll make the most of me while you're at it."

"Who made *you* so cynical?" he grinned.

"That Strip we were talking about. Where everyone smiles all the time because everyone is so frightened all the time—they are so frightened that they'll lose what they have, or never get what they want, that they'll bargain with anything, from body to soul."

"Would *you?*"

"Are you asking me if I *will?*"

"No. I want to know if you'd go to bed with me so that I'd help you get what you want in the business. Consider it a hypothetical question."

"Hypothetically, I might. I want a career bad enough."

"You don't sound too convincing."

"I suppose not. Let's not put a premium on sex. If you're having sex because you're in love—or because you want babies—that's one thing. If you want sex because your body is hungry, that's another thing. Maybe I'm young, but I'm old enough to know that women were prostituting themselves to get what they wanted long before we had motion pictures and the industry."

"That's quite a speech."

She laughed a little at herself, and at the quizzical expression upon his face. She had not meant to say so much, and abruptly she hadn't the slightest idea where the talk had taken them.

"I wonder what happened to Clint and Carla?" she said.

Even as she spoke, as if on cue, a door chime sounded.

"They must have heard me," she smiled.

A quick flash of annoyance crossed Nytrack's face and abruptly Kima knew that he had not expected the couple, that this was not according to plan. Probably Clint—an inveterate partier after a few drinks—had decided to join them, after all. Nytrack quickly erased his frown.

"I'll let them in," he said.

He left her and she waited to hear Clint's voice. Instead, she heard a woman's voice that she did not immediately recognize. It was a strident angry voice: "Someone called me, that's how I know! Someone saw you leave with her."

"Don't jump to conclusions," Nytrack's voice snapped.

Kima stared at the entrance to the room as Marianne Thurlow stormed in. It was the first time that she had seen the star off screen and she realized that Marianne was indeed a beautiful woman. Her dark, red hair seemed alive with highlights. Her gray-green eyes flashed with anger. She wore a light coat loosely draped over sweater-covered shoulders and tight Capri pants. Obviously she had been lounging at home when she had received the call that had angered her. Now the sweater only served to accentuate the fullness of her bosom, and the tightness of the Capris pants empasized the angry tenseness of her whole body.

The star stopped and glared at Kima, so that Kima felt a moment of panic from the sheer intensity of anger in the other woman's eyes.

"Who are you?" Marianne demanded.

Nytrack took command of the situation. "Kima, this is Marianne Thurlow—Marianne ... Kima Shannon."

Marianne turned to Nytrack with a thin smile that was almost a triumphant sneer. "I never heard of her!" Then, as if she had taken a second evaluation of Kima, her temper flared again. "How *dare* you do this to me, Ken Nytrack? With a cheap little chippy who—"

"That's enough," Nytrack interrupted sharply. "Miss Shannon is from New York. She's an experienced actress and—"

"Experienced *actress?*" Marianne laughed. "I'll bet she's experienced! In bed! Is she good, Ken?"

"Shut up!" Nytrack said.

The redheaded woman stared at him and evidently sensed that she had gone too far. Their eyes held for a few seconds, and finally she looked down.

"Don't push it," Nytrack said quietly. "Don't push it, Marianne. You've had a good thing. Take care of it."

"But you and I—I mean, you've no *right*, Ken, you've no *right!*"

He regarded her without expression. "Don't make a fool of yourself," he said. "This is business. I want to talk with Miss Shannon about a role in *Ground Rules.*"

"Oh?" Marianne's eyes still reflected her suspicion, but she had her anger under control. She realized that he was giving her a small shred of face-saving grace.

Nytrack watched her with a small smile of amusement, as if he enjoyed her sudden discomfort. "I know," he finally said. "The place and time are unusual, but Miss Shannon is under contract to someone else. We have to work behind the scenes."

Marianne accepted the out for what it was worth.

"Oh," she said again. "I didn't realize. Don't blame me too much, Ken. This friend called and—"

"All right. Let's just forget it. You go home and get some sleep. Kima and I still have some contract problems to discuss."

Marianne hesitated a fraction of a moment and then nodded. She turned to Kima and smiled coldly. "Good night, Miss Shannon," she said. There was a trace of pure mockery in her voice, and despite the star's attempted smile, Kima recognized a look of unadulterated hatred.

Marianne turned and went out with Ken Nytrack. Kima heard the door close and after a few moments Nytrack rejoined her. He mixed fresh drinks and brought one to her, standing before her.

"I'm sorry about that," he said. "Marianne's—shall we say, impulsive? Emotional?"

Kima smiled. "Proprietary might be better."

Nytrack laughed. "All right, so we've called one spade a spade, let's try another."

"All right. Let's."

"You're a lovely, exciting, desirable girl. If you had everything that you could possibly want, and if I could do absolutely nothing for you in the way of career, wealth, or stature, I'd still want to take you to bed. If I were a truck driver, a hard rock miner, an insurance salesman—anything—I'd want to go to bed with you."

"That sounds almost like a proposal!" she said wryly.

"It does, but it isn't," he smiled. "I wasn't actually asking you to bed with me—I was just telling you why I *might*."

"Fair enough."

"Work tomorrow?"

"No. I've a day off."

"Stand up."

She hesitated, looking at him thoughtfully, and then she obediently stood. He took her shoulders in his hands and after a moment he kissed her. It was a hard, commanding kiss and Kima knew that never before had she been kissed in such a way, that never before had she been so shaken by a kiss. He held her away from him.

"I promise you nothing tangible," he said. "No contract. No part in a picture. Nothing but the way I seem to feel about you, and that may be completely transient. Am I being clear?"

"Yes."

"All right. Will you go to bed with me?"

She remembered her preparations for just such a contingency, and abruptly she felt a tremendous surge of shame. She had almost decided to comply with his possible request even before she had come on the date with him! She actually had come prepared to go to bed with him; she had deliberately safeguarded herself against pregnancy.

She remembered the scene that Marianne had made, and she wondered how much of her sudden shame she could lay to Marianne's insinuations.

It isn't that, she thought. *She didn't make the difference. I simply will not be easy. I won't be. There has to be more.*

But even as she realized her own strength, she also recognized that Ken Nytrack's kiss had shaken her. She never could be too certain of the future with him now.

"No," she said. "I won't go to bed with you."

He smiled. "All right," he said. "No bedding down. We'll talk about it again sometime. But you can stay all night."

"I don't think I'd better."

"We can have a few more drinks, some talk, some music. It's late and a long drive to your place," he said. He smiled again and added, "The bedrooms all have locks. The kind that bolt."

His smile was contagious. No matter what his eventual plans might be, she had no worry about his immediate ones. She could never imagine him breaking down doors or attempting rape!

"All right," she said. "I'll sleep here. Alone."

"Alone," he said. "Regretfully.... alone!" He raised his glass in a small toast, and they both laughed.

CHAPTER FIVE

W HEN SHE FOUND the dining room, Ken Nytrack was at a breakfast table talking into a telephone. She hesitated in the doorway, unavoidably listening to the conversation.

"I know I've a starting date four weeks away. I know how long it takes to fly to Italy and get things lined up. Don't tell me things I know. And I won't be leaving here tomorrow. I've changed my plans. The starting date stands. We'll have a new girl. I'm going to take a long shot—like I did with *Corner Games.* It worked then, and I think it will now. Line up as much as you can there in Rome. Okay?"

He listened for a few moments with a brief "yes" or "no" and finally said, "Kima Shannon. You don't know her. I've a hell of a lot of work to do with her, but I think she has what we want for *Ground Rules*—a good contrast against Marianne and she'll complement Glasgow.... Yes, she's under contract to PAK—I'll handle that. Right. Call you tomorrow."

He put down the telephone and looked across the room at Kima.

"Hi!" he smiled. "Sleep well?"

"Fine!"

He indicated a chair at the table. "I'll have Joe fix you breakfast."

"Joe?"

"Houseboy. He's been with me a long time. Joe Wong. He already knows you're here."

She smiled. It didn't mattter. A houseboy was a houseboy, and houseboys in Hollywood probably knew more Hollywood history than anyone. And Joe probably knew that she had slept alone.

"Ken—I heard some of your call."

"Understand what I was talking about?"

"I think so," she said in her blunt, slightly academic voice that she sometimes used to mask emotions. "I think you were telling someone in Rome that you want to use me in a new picture called *Ground Rules*. That I would play opposite someone called Glasgow—and that could only mean Rick Glasgow. And there was something about taking care of my contract with PAK. That's the main part—except that I'm also a long shot and need to do a lot of hard work."

"You got the main points," he said. "Incidentally, who's your agent?"

"Milo Ginz. But don't call him until we've talked. I want to know what this is all about."

"Fair enough. But breakfast first."

He touched a floor button and a middle-aged Oriental came in. Nytrack suggested juice, eggs, toast and coffee. Kima nodded and the houseboy left them.

Obviously in this household luxury and service were taken for granted. The shower stall in the bathroom adjoining her bedroom was almost as large as the full bathroom in her apartment. On a dressing table in a tray were an unwrapped toothbrush, a new tube of toothpaste, and a small assortment of essential cosmetics. Another plain box was sealed in cellophane. She had opened it and blushed when she saw the implement for "feminine hygiene" tucked inside.

"The voice of experience," she had said aloud, and then had laughed and taken a quick shower.

Now she and Ken made small talk for the surprisingly few moments it took for the houseboy to bring her breakfast. Nytrack poured coffee for her and she ate. When she finished, he lit a cigarette for her.

"All right," he said. "Now the questions."

"How right was I about things?"

"All the way down the line. I bought the story six months ago. It's an original by Bart Pobello. Better than *Corner Games*, and it cost me three hundred thousand—and worth it. As you guessed, I'm using Rick Glasgow—he's getting half a million a job now. Marianne is getting a big share. It's a high-cost production and—"

"Maybe you shouldn't talk such fabulous amounts to me," she said. "I'll want some. Even if I know you'll have to teach me a lot, and that you're taking a long shot on me, I'll—" She shrugged and grinned. "Or shouldn't I be talking this way?"

"What's PAK paying you? Three a week?"

"Two-fifty. With taxes and all that out—plus agent—with a retainer to Sam—"

"Sam?"

"A friend. Press agent. I don't pay him much—anyhow, there's not much left."

"PAK is cheap. But you're under contract. I'm glad you worry about what you earn. I don't like stupid women. You're not stupid."

"Thank you, sir."

"We'll have to do something about PAK. Mind if I call Milo?"

"What girl would, under the circumstances?"

He smoked in silence for a moment. "Let me talk frankly," he said. "Not as I might with some girls. With you, I have a hunch that frankness is better."

She saw the seriousness in his eyes. "I wish you *would* be frank."

"Do you know what the so-called protégé system is out here?"

"You mean about getting into pictures?"

"Let's start with basics. How do you get in pictures? Most experts agree that there are several ways."

"Besides casting couches?"

"Don't wisecrack." He smiled the edge off his words. "For instance, you can be born into the business. A lot of second-generation people are in top spots, and third and fourth are beginning to show up."

"You mean the family affair—like the Cohns at Columbia?"

"There's hardly a major studio that doesn't have relatives in important places. And it goes on in the acting ranks. You can name them—the old-timers' kids who are getting good roles. And producers—20th Century with Richard Zanuck, son of Darryl—along with Plato Skouras, son of Spyros."

"I know. All the sons, daughters, uncles, aunts, cousins, in-laws—and, I've heard, this may include the mistresses. Is that what you're getting at?"

"Let me finish. There's another way. This is the protégé method. A producer or director or studio executive spots a good-looking girl. She may be anywhere—a drive-in, a campus, an amateur production, a teen-age dance session, TV—anywhere. And it may be a boy as well as a girl. So the high and mighty likes—and reaches. God knows how many times this is a sex urge. Probably in most cases. At any rate, it begins."

"The protégé bit?"

He nodded. "They buy young sex. They want to keep it around and they pay for it. So quite a few of these kids get started on the star-production line. They get drama coaching, voice coaching, publicity, small parts, grooming, larger parts, more publicity, polishing, better parts, more grooming, more publicity—hell, you know the story. Sometimes they even become stars. But meanwhile a lot of real talent may get stepped on, ignored and shoved aside."

"That's how I heard it was," Kima said. "But how *about* talent? What about the people who have it?"

"That's possibly the third important way to make the grade. And the tough way. Sometimes a world of talent won't get you half as much as a well-filled bra and willingness to take it off for the right man."

"Are you going to make a point with all this discussion?"

"Yes. I think you have talent. I've watched you. I've talked with some people. I respect Solly's opinion. Pat Sahnstein will never get an Oscar—or an Emmie—but he does an honest job most of the time. He likes your work."

Nytrack paused to light another cigarette.

"You see," he continued, "no matter how many relatives you have around, or how many protégés with no real talent, you still have to have *some* talent to do a good picture—even a good TV segment. And to make Oscar-winning productions, you usually have to have a *great deal* of talent working for you. I'm interested in talent."

Kima thought about his words, gazing into his lean, serious face.

"Now I'm confused," she said. "You evidently are offering me a lot. But are you offering it because you want me for a protégé—as you've painted them—or does talent have something to do with it?"

"Possibly both," he said. "Now I'm going to call Milo Ginz and see what we can do about your contract."

He reached for the telephone. Kima watched him, thinking about his words, and a little startled by all that had been said.

There was no smog and the late afternoon sun still was warm upon the water in the large pool and the adjoining patio. Someone in the household had found a swim suit for her, and Kima stretched on a sun pad, looking toward the rambling house where Ken Nytrack had gone a few moments before.

Sitting in a deck chair beside her, Milo Ginz stared solemnly at her through thick eyeglasses. He was a small, wizened, extremely unattractive man who wore expensively tailored suits, custom shirts, impeccable ties and one-hundred-dollar shoes to offset his lack of physical attributes. In his sixties, and a product of early, roughshod days in the business, he handled some of the finest talent.

"They won't like it at PAK," he said. "They don't know yet what maybe they got in you. When they find out who wants you, they're not going to like it if we get out easy before they can gouge somebody."

"Can you do it, Mr. Ginz?"

"Call me Milo, darling. To girls like you I am Milo. Now, maybe we can do it. I got ways. But I'm thinking if Ken Nytrack wants you this bad, maybe he wants more than what he's quoting."

"I don't think so. It isn't too important a part. Rick Glasgow and Marianne Thurlow get the top billing."

Ginz blinked solemnly behind his thick glasses. "You let me do the thinking, darling. That's why you pay me. I'll see what I can do. But I got to ask you a question, Kima."

"Ask."

"You sure you want to get into this?"

"Into what?"

Ginz shrugged his thin shoulders and motioned to the grounds and mansion. "Like this. You know about him, Kima?"

"Should I?"

"Don't be innocent with me, darling. Please? You been out here long enough to know how it is. Advice I feel I got to give along with service when I got a property like you. And I'm your friend. You know that Milo Ginz, your agent, also is your friend?"

She looked into his unattractive face and saw that he meant his words. She recognized a true rapport between her and this ugly little man who had a reputation for shrewdness, ability and a strange and fierce loyalty to his clients.

"Yes, Milo. I know you're my friend. And I think I know what you're trying to say. But perhaps you'd better spell it out for me."

"I got only a few things to tell you, darling. Like this man Nytrack is great. You've seen his pictures and maybe the Oscars. You know he's got money? More than you think. Like Howard Hughes, maybe. Who knows? And you know you don't hear much about him and women. He was married and she's a nice girl. I like her. He got bitter when they split up. Seldom I've seen anyone so bitter. Then he made like he got over it. Maybe you haven't heard much about his women since, but they've been here."

"So?"

"So where are they now? What's happened to them?"

"Marianne did pretty well in *Corner Games* and afterward."

"Real good. And even if he aces her out for you, she'll do all right. I know two studios want her. She's got it made for a while. But there's a difference between you and her, Kima."

"She had more experience and—"

"No, no. That's not what I mean."

"What are you trying to tell me?"

"The girls he keeps here, like it might be shaping up for you— and I'm no prude, darling—well, the girls who fit that place in his life, they're not like you. So you got to be careful and remember."

"Remember what, Milo?"

"That he can be a real nice guy," said Ginz. "And he can be a son-of-a-bitch. Don't ever cross him. He's full of drive, ability, talent, charm, strength—he's got more than any three men usually have. But he wants things to work his way. Don't ever forget."

"But, Milo, he's offered me a part in his picture. You're here to make a deal."

Ginz lit a cigarette and stared at the glowing coal on the tip.

"That's what makes this different, Kima. Maybe you've got something the others didn't have. I just want to tell you. It's up to you. I can't advise you to turn down money like that—if you think you can handle everything else."

She reached for his cigarettes and lighter and lit a cigarette. Slowly she exhaled the smoke, her expression thoughtful.

"I'm going to take the chance, Milo," she said.

"Okay. That's that. I'll do my best for you."

"For *us*, Milo," she smiled.

"If a nice girl like you is going to get hurt bad, the money I don't need that much," Milo Ginz said.

Nytrack was coming across the broad expanse of lawn. He wore swim trunks and loafers. He was frowning as he rejoined them.

"Sorry to take so long," he said. "It was an important call." He sat in a chair beside Ginz and gave Kima a glance of amusement. "Was Milo telling you what a son-of-a-bitch I can be?"

She laughed. "His exact words!"

Nytrack looked at Ginz. "Roughly ten weeks of production time. Where else can you get her two thousand a week right now?"

Ginz shrugged elaborately. He looked at Kima and nodded.

"Am I objecting?" she smiled.

Nytrack said to the agent. "Can you spring her from PAK?"

"I think so—in one way or another."

"I don't care how you do it. Maybe you get her on loan as a starter and we figure a way to spring her later. The point is I need her now."

"If they can make a buck, and we say it's a bit part, maybe we can do it that way," Ginz said.

"Okay. I'll stretch a point. I want her to get the twenty grand gross for the picture. I'll up it. She's getting two-fifty a week from them. I'll settle for three-fifty on loan. Will they play?"

"They'll play," Ginz said softly. "I can swing another trade for a lover boy they want next month. I'll wheel and deal."

Nytrack turned his attention back to Kima. "How much more do you have in the *Methuselah* series?"

"Maybe a couple of days," Ginz answered for her. "They wrote her into what was left of the series. They might simply write her out again."

"You'll handle that, too?" Nytrack asked Ginz.

"Yes. Sahnstein and I are close. I'm married to his sister."

"Okay, then. Kima, starting tomorrow you go to work. Drama coach, voice—the full treatment. I want something done about your hair, too. You need a new look for this role. I've a script in the house. You can start studying at once."

He looked at the small agent. "All set then?"

"Set," Ginz said. He stood and put out his cigarette. "You got company," he said, nodding toward the house.

Clint Clinton and Carla Flaxon were coming toward them. Their voices were edging into the boisterous tones inspired by alcohol, and they had a telltale carelessness of walk.

"Hi!" Clint yelled. "Hi!"

The threesome by the pool watched them approach. A frown of annoyance crossed Nytrack's face again, but he erased it almost instantly.

"Looks like you haven't stopped since last night," he smiled.

"Oh, we did," Clinton said solemnly, one arm around the blonde starlet as they stopped beside the pool. "Late to work, but we finished early this afternoon. Sahnstein's hacked at me again. So to hell with him." Clint carefully lit a cigarette. "Then baby and I got smashed! Real, crazy smashed. Me'n my ring-a-ding-ding baby!"

Carla slipped from under his arm and smiled at Nytrack, ignored Milo Ginz after a quick glance, and looked at Kima, who still was stretched out on the sun pad.

"Still on your back, dear?" Carla asked.

Kima felt quick anger and almost got up, but Carla already had turned away, a little unsteadily, and was looking at the water and giggling. Whatever she had been drinking had been powerful.

"Goin' swimmin'!" she announced.

With a quick movement she stripped off her blouse, stepped out of her skirt, and kicked off her shoes. She wore nothing under the skirt and was clad only in a brassiere. She reached behind her, unsnapped it and shrugged the straps over her shoulders. It dropped. She had turned her back to the men, and now she glanced over a shoulder.

"Look, boys," she said. "Really a blonde! " She revolved slowly and displayed her nudity to the three men without glancing at Kima. Then she turned and plunged into the water.

"Ring-a-ding-ding baby!" Clinton shouted. Fully clad, he plunged into the water. They swam furiously toward the far end of the pool where he caught her and they went into a splashing, violent, noisy struggle and embrace.

Ken Nytrack watched them, his smile even thinner and more forced.

"Come on," he said to Kima and the thin little agent. "I'll send someone down with dinner for them and to look after them."

Abruptly he looked at Kima and his smile somehow become transformed into one of genuine enthusiasm and pleasure.

"Change of plans," he said. "You don't have to work tomorrow. We'll take a break first."

She got up from the pad with questioning eyes.

"We're going to fly to Vegas," he told her. He turned to Ginz. "Want to come, Milo?"

"Not me, Ken. I got work to do."

At the far end of the pool Carla shrieked in feigned alarm. "Not here, Clint! Not here!"

"Ring-a-ding-ding!" Clint shouted. "Got a ring-a-ding-ding baby!"

"Stop it, Clint! Stop it—Oh, goddamn you, Clint! Right here in the pool where everyone can see … ! "

But no one was watching. Kima and Ken and Milo Ginz already were halfway to the house.

CHAPTER SIX

S HE NEVES HAD BEEN in Las Vegas. Now, an hour before midnight, and a few hours after their arrival, she began to understand the strange excitement that brought so many to the desert city.

Ken Nytrack had managed things with the efficiency that she was beginning to take for granted in his fastpaced way of life. They had flown to the Nevada city in a chartered plane. Rooms in one of the most plush hotels were ready for them. A women's exclusive shop was open and he had helped her select a dress and some casuals for a short stay. They had not bothered to stop at her apartment before leaving.

They had eaten and enjoyed a minor extravaganza that the management called a "floor show" and had strolled into a gaming room. For the first time she heard the noises that are singularly germane to gambling casinos: the click of chips, voices of housemen, and in the background the constant whir of slot machines.

Ken handed her a pile of chips. "Play them where you like," he told her. "I'm going to try the dice."

"Can't I come with you?"

"My one superstition," he said. "I never want my girl with me when I'm shooting craps. Crazy?"

With amusement she saw a slight embarrassment in his face. This was the first time she had seen a weakness in him.

"I understand," she smiled. "These chips—how much?"

"Ten dollars each. You have fifty. Here's another five hundred in currency for walk-around money and more chips if you need them." He gave her the folded money. She tried to refuse.

"Ken, I don't know anything about gambling. I mean—"

"You're going to meet a friend of mine. He'll look after you."

"But isn't that—well, I'm here with *you* and—"

"I'll get the gambling out of my system in a few hours. I've set twenty thousand for tonight—I'll either double or go broke."

"Then why don't you bet just once? Double or nothing?"

"Your trouble is practicality," he laughed. "You're right, of course. Only I like to shoot craps."

"You're a little complex sometimes," she smiled. "Where is this friend of yours? I want to learn how to play roulette."

"Over there having a drink. Come on and meet him."

The man probably was in his mid-thirties. He was well built and had the trim, alert look that Ken Nytrack had. His black hair was cut very short. His eyes were as dark as Kima's. When he smiled his teeth were even and white.

"Kima, this is Bill Rold," Nytrack said. "Bill ... Kima Shannon. Teach her to play roulette and show her the town!"

Rold looked at Kima with frank, appraising eyes. He smiled and the calculating look in his eyes vanished. He became friendly—a good-looking young man being very pleasant. "Fine," he nodded. "Good luck."

A little puzzled by the whole thing, Kima watched Ken Nytrack leave them. At her elbow Rold chuckled.

"He's a gambler," he said. "He could be one of the great ones. Even in business he likes the big gambles."

"I'm one of his long shots," Kima said wryly.

Rold smiled. "I'd take some of that action myself."

Kima glanced at him archly. "Maybe Ken should check his watchdogs a little more closely. That's almost a pass."

"I'm not a watchdog. I'm a friend, and he wants you to enjoy yourself. Shall we go?"

"Where?"

"It's near midnight—the magic floor show hour. Most of the last ones for the night start then. What would you like to see?"

"What is there?"

"Well, Danny Kaye is at the Desert Inn, Philippine Festival at the Dunes and if you like Al Hirt's trumpet, it's there, too. Over at the Flamingo are Joe E. Louis and Vic Damone. If you like nudes, the New Frontier. The Riviera has a good show, or you can catch some of Sinatra's clan at the Sands. The Folies-Bergere at the Tropicana, and—"

"Do you work for the Chamber of Commerce or a theatrical booking agency?" Kima laughed.

"You'd be surprised what I do for a living."

"Maybe you're a member of the syndicate. Or is there really one?"

"There are interests."

"Just what *do* you do?"

"I own a small piece of this showplace where you're staying," he said. "I make most of my money in Hollywood handling tax problems."

"Handling tax problems!"

"Don't laugh, beautiful. I started out to be an attorney. Somewhere along the line things happened. In a business where the government can end up taking more than ninety percent of what you earn—show business—it pays to have someone around who knows the tax angles."

"I suppose so."

"Eventually maybe you'll be trying to find a way to take your salary in capital gains—trading your talent for shares in a corporation—even living and working abroad so that you can manage to keep something of what you earn during the few years you probably can stay on the top."

"And you help people with matters like this?"

"Only certain people. That's my specialty—that and helping operate this place a little, and giving advice, and taking care of my friends' girls when my friends are busy shooting craps."

"Don't you have some girls of your own to take care of?"

"Sometimes. I play the field. Shall we go?"

"Have you decided where?"

"We'll take a tour. That may be more fun. He'll still be at that crap table three hours from now if I know him and the way he plays."

Whatever Bill Rold's ability as a tax consultant might be, he was an accomplished guide, host and good-time companion. By two o'clock Kima was impressed by what she had seen and slightly dizzy from the drinks she had consumed.

They returned to the table where Ken Nytrack stood, a pile of chips in front of him, his attention completely centered upon the play. He hardly seemed to notice that they had returned.

"How's the play?" Rold asked.

"Better than even and it's beginning to break for me."

"Then you don't want to quit?"

"No. Okay with you two?" He smiled at them and put a careless arm about Kima for a few seconds, even as he placed a bet on the table. "Win anything, Kima?"

"A little. I learned how to play roulette, we saw a good show and—"

"Fine! Look, Bill, is anything working tonight?"

"A party in one of the guest houses—some of the Hollywood crowd and show people from around town. Mike York is throwing it."

"Why don't I meet you there in a couple of hours?" Nytrack turned his attention back to the game.

Bill Rold led Kima away. "The difference," he said, "is that I wouldn't trust you with me."

"Aren't you safe?"

"I'm a male," he grinned. "Come on. We'll go to this blast. It should be a real gasser."

"A Clyde?"

"As Sinatra or the Pack might say, a Clyde."

The "guest house" was much larger than she had expected to see. The party was in full swing when they arrived. Drinks were abundant. Voices, music, laughter, shrieks, giggles and guffaws created a party cacophony. Kima recognized an unusual number of Broadway and Hollywood personalities. No one seemed to bother with introductions. The simple fact that one was there seemed to be introduction enough—and excuse enough for almost any familiarity.

Occasionally Rold appeared and then disappeared. Strangers seemed to become friends in seconds, and always there was a filled glass.

Kima felt the mounting effects of her drinks. Inhibitions began to drop away. She flirted with a Broadway star and lightly returned his kiss, indifferent when he abandoned her for a passing blonde. She danced with a swarthy man who looked like a gangster. A tall, broad man replaced her empty glass with a full one.

"I don't know you," he said.

"I know you," Kima smiled triumphantly, sampling the drink. She felt dizzy and put a hand on him to steady herself. "You're Tom Darman, fastest gun on TV! You're the hero!"

"Star of the westerns—that's me," he grinned. "Just lookin' fer a purty little filly like you. 'N mighty purty you are, ma'am!"

"Don't mind if I do," Kima giggled, not having the slightest idea why she had spoken the sentence. She sipped again at her drink.

"Reckon as how I wouldn't mind either," the tall actor responded, swaying a little. "How come a chick like you never's been on our show? You in the business?"

Solemnly Kima said, "I am a trained actress."

"Let's talk about this," he said. "Like maybe I could get you a role or two in a segment or two for a buck or two." He grinned and finished his drink. "Come on."

Taking her hand, he guided her through the crowd to a bar and got fresh drinks for them. Still clasping her hand, he pulled her on a jostled trail toward a hallway.

Obediently she followed him. It had been a long night with a great many drinks and by now anything seemed logical—even walking down this hallway with a TV star she had seen only on a screen before this night.

He took her to a bedroom and closed the door. A lamp lighted an empty double bed. Someone had left two glasses on a bedside table. The bedspread was rumpled, the pillows heavily indented. Two cigarette stubs, one lipstick stained, lay in an ashtray, a single bobby pin on the rumpled spread.

Darman sat on the bed and pulled Kima down beside him. He looked seriously at his drink and finally drank it in long, decisive swallows. He put down the glass and turned to her.

"What's your name?" he said.

"Kima Shannon."

He took her glass and put it beside his. He held her in the circle of an arm, forced her back upon the bed, and kissed her long and hard.

Instinctively she fought against him and managed to squirm away and to sit up. A wedge of sobriety forced itself into her consciousness and she sensed that she was in danger.

"No," she said. "Tom—let's not get involved. Okay?"

He was sitting again and his smile was replaced with an ugly expression that frightened her.

"It was your idea," he said angrily. "You made the play."

"You misunderstood me, Tom. Really! Look—let's not get in a thing about it? Let's go back to the party?"

"Like hell! We're here on a bed, and we're going to use it."

She tried to get up but he pulled her back.

"Let me go, Tom! I mean it!"

"When I'm finished," he said. "When I'm finished, baby."

Desperately and silently she fought him. She bit and scratched and once he cried out in pain. He slapped her and her senses reeled. A hand pulled at the hem of her dress. His weight was heavy upon her. Instinctively she tried to withdraw her hips, to roll and turn. She felt his masculine pursuit become relentless and harsh.

"No! ... No! ..." Her scream was smothered by his mouth. She struggled in a sudden outburst of panic.

Abruptly he left her, as if a powerful claw had clamped upon his back and lifted him away. He sprawled upon the floor and Kima saw another man in the room. He was closing the door, his back to her. He turned. It was Bill Rold. Automatically she pulled down her dress.

"You've had too much to drink," he said curtly.

"Bill! I didn't come here with him to—I mean—"

"I know—you were fighting him off. But you *did* come in here with him. What did you expect? You're a big girl."

"It wasn't like that! I didn't—"

There was no time to say more. Darman was on his feet. He shook his head angrily as if to clear it, and stood with legs apart, fists doubled, glaring at Rold.

"What the hell's wrong with you, Rold?" he snapped.

"You picked the wrong girl, Tom."

"What do you mean, *picked?* It was her idea. She made a play for me. And I'll be damned if you're going to stop it!"

He advanced upon the smaller man. Rold alertly shifted his weight forward and his hands came out from his sides. "Take it easy, Tom. She's not for you. Just forget it."

"You nosy bastard!" Darman growled. "You *work* for me, tax man. You take my dough. Don't tell *me* who I'm going to lay! Now get the hell out of here and close the door after you."

"Knock it off, chum. You're gassed. Kima and I'll forget it. Let's all go back to the party."

Kima got up from the bed and took a step toward Rold. The TV star turned toward her.

"Get back on that bed," he snarled. "I mean it, baby!"

"Tom—no. Bill's right. Let's go back to the party and—"

He slapped her again. The blow sent her staggering back.

Bill Rold moved toward Darman. His left fist flashed out and snapped Darman's head back. Rold followed with a hard right, but Darman turned his head and took the blow on a cheek.

Cursing steadily, Darman began to swing wildly, forcing the smaller man back with the brute strength of his onslaught.

Rold ducked, weaved and blocked. A blow caught him on the side of his head and he staggered. A chair went over. Darman sprang on him and they crashed to the floor. The star jerked a knee upward, trying to find Rold's groin. He landed a right to the side of Rold's mouth and Rold rolled and scrambled away.

They got to their feet. Both men were breathing hard. A trickle of blood edged from the corner of Rold's lips. Darman swung a hard right and missed. The blow carried him forward and Rold shot a short, jolting jab into the star's midriff. Darman gasped and staggered, bending over.

Rold sidestepped neatly and brought the side of his right hand down on the back of Darman's neck in a judo chop.

Darman sprawled face down on the floor, motionless. Rold wiped blood from his mouth with a handkerchief. He tidied his necktie and tucked in his shirt, ignoring both the fallen man and Kima. Finally he put away his handkerchief and looked at her.

"Okay," he said shortly. "Let's go."

She nodded silently, still frightened by the violence she had just witnessed, abashed that she had been the cause.

"Is he all right?" she asked.

"He's all right," Rold said. Darman was trying to get to his hands and knees. He managed to get to the bed and sit on it. He glared balefully at Rold.

"You're fired," he said.

"Okay," Rold nodded. "So I'm fired. Good night, Tom. You'd better clean up before you go back to the party."

He took Kima's hand and led her out of the bedroom into the hallway, closing the door after him.

"Bill," Kima said, "I'm sorry. I've probably lost you a client."

"He'll get over it."

"And, Bill—thanks. You arrived just in time. Like the Marines, or Eliot Ness, or somebody." She felt better now. She put a hand on one of his arms. "Really, Bill. I mean thanks an awful lot. I was so frightened. You take good care of Ken Nytrack's girl."

"I didn't do it for Ken," Rold said. "It was for you." He was looking at her with a trace of anger that matched the tone of his voice. "You didn't have to go into the bedroom with him. You didn't have to—oh, skip it. You're Nytrack's girl."

Their eyes locked for a silent moment, until she turned away.

"When will Ken be here?" she asked. "I don't believe I like this party very well."

"He's not coming. He's still at the table. He called. That's why I began looking for you and someone said he saw you and Darman heading toward the bedrooms."

"What do we do now?"

"Stay at the party. Or call it a night. Whatever you like. There's more town to see—plenty of action. Or maybe you're hungry."

"That's the best idea. Ham and eggs?"

"Okay."

It was no plush place where he took her. The café looked old and the customers appeared to be town people. The food was very good.

As they ate, she felt sobriety steadily returning to her. When they finished, she accepted a cigarette. Rold glanced at his watch.

"Almost four," he said. "It's been a night."

She studied him more closely, suddenly aware of his clean, strong features and the charm of his smile.

"Pass inspection?" he asked, his anger apparently gone.

"I just hadn't really looked at you before. Do you think Ken has finished gambling?"

"Possibly. Or he may stay for hours."

"I guess I don't understand him very well."

"How long have you known him?"

"I'm almost ashamed to admit—I met him last night. I guess it was last night. It seems longer. So much has happened."

Rold's eyebrows went up and his look of skepticism angered her.

"Don't get the wrong idea," she said. "I'm no pick-up tramp."

"Who said so?" He stared at her intently for a moment and then shrugged. "It could happen that way with him.

He lives it up fast. Very fast. I'm sorry if I offended you."

"All right," she said, after a brief hesitation. "I don't suppose there'd be any reason for you to think otherwise. The way it looks."

"That's not true. I didn't have to find you in the so-called nick-of-time."

She realized that he was telling the truth. "I'm sorry, Bill."

"You're Ken Nytrack's girl. Let's not forget that."

"Is his brand upon a girl that important?"

"Don't be flip with what you've managed to get. You're slated for a good part in the picture. It could make you. Ken thinks you have real talent. What's between you two personally is up to you. Usually he doesn't mix business with pleasure."

"Am I pleasure?"

"Our TV star wasn't kidding," Bill smiled. "He wanted. So could a lot of men. Including Ken." He hesitated. "Okay—incuding me."

"That's close to being a pass."

"The conversation is becoming stupid," he said. "We're going."

They returned to the casino just in time to meet Nytrack leaving the table. He welcomed them with a broad smile.

"Hi! Have a good time, you two? I made sixty grand here."

"Real good," Kima smiled. "Bill's nice."

"He's a good tax man, too," Nytrack said. He put an arm around Kima's shoulders. "Like her, Bill?"

Rold smiled, but he obviously had taken particular notice of the affectionate arm, and his eyes failed to echo the smile.

"Just fine," he nodded. "She'll be good in *Ground Rules*."

Ken nodded, his typical smile of amusement tugging at the corners of his mouth as he glanced from Rold to Kima and back to the man. "A real property," he said.

"Yes," Rold said evenly. "A real property." He smiled at Kima. "It's been fun."

Kima caught the play on the word "property" and almost blushed. She smiled at Bill Rold. "Thanks, Bill—for everything."

"As I said, it's been fun. And thanks, Ken, for the loan of your—property?" He tempered the minor *double-entendre* with a smile.

Nytrack returned the smile. "See you later."

Kima and Nytrack watched the dark, slim man leave them.

"He liked you," Ken said.

"I like him," she nodded. "He's nice, Ken. Really nice."

"He not only likes you, but he wants you. And I don't blame him."

"You're imagining things," Kima protested lightly.

"I don't imagine things like this—not the relationships between people in real life," he told her. "I reserve imagination for the screen. I know when a man goes for a woman. He goes for you." Ken laughed softly. "Don't look so worried. I can't blame another man for wanting the woman I also want. If a woman is desirable, more than one man will certainly want her."

Kima remembered the TV star and the bedroom. Abruptly she wished Ken would talk about something else, but she knew that his thoughts were centered now upon her and his desires— or upon his desires and her. She thought that his desire might be much more important to him than was she.

"Too sleepy to talk a while?" he asked.

She wondered where the talk might lead, and she was apprehensive. However, she had come to Las Vegas with him. She was his guest. She was going to be in his picture. Certainly she could talk with him.

"If you're not," she said.

He shook his head. "Let's go up. Go to your room and get into something comfortable and come to mine. It's larger. I want to talk about your role in *Ground Rules*. It may take a while."

Twenty minutes later she knocked softly at his door. She had put on a sweater and skirt—casuals he had bought for her when they arrived. He opened the door. He wore slacks and a shirt open at the throat. Drinks were on a table in front of a sofa.

He looked her over, as a director might quickly check the appearance of an actress coming on a set. "You look good in sweaters," he said. "You have a good body." He led her to the sofa and handed a drink to her.

"I don't know." she hesitated. "I've already drunk a lot, Ken."

"It's fine Scotch," he smiled. "Really good. Try it."

She did and agreed with him. Only the most expensive Scotch had the taste and aroma of the drink she held.

"I want to talk about us," he said abruptly. "How I feel about you."

She finished some of the drink and looked across the top of the glass at him. The drink was strong. Something always seemed to happen when she had strong drinks. Something to do with inhibitions, and candor, and impulsiveness. Now she felt the urge for candid talk.

"Ken, how *do* you feel about me?" she asked. "You brought me here—and turned me over to another man. You intimated to him—with double-talk—that I'm your property. I'm not. You learned that last night."

He nodded. "If it had been any other way, you wouldn't be here. You're here because I respect you."

"That's almost a cliché."

He shrugged. "I'm not trying to make smart talk. Just admitting a truth. First, I was attracted to you. Then I wanted you. Usually I get what I want. Last night I didn't. So I had to back up and take a second look. I brought us here. And I had to be away from you—temporarily—to think it through. So I gambled. Gambling eases everything else from my mind. When I stop—return to reality—sometimes I find that my problems are solved. It happened tonight."

"And what answer did you find?"

"That you're my woman. I want you and need you. And if that adds up to love, then I love you."

"And Marianne?"

"A fair question deserving an honest answer. Nothing. Forget she exists. It didn't have anything to do with you and me before we met—it doesn't now. This is between us. You're my woman. Is that clear? You're my woman."

"Don't I have anything to say about it?"

"Last night I asked you to stand up—and I kissed you." "I remember."

"Let's try again. Stand up."

She looked up at him and her curiosity became intensely alive. All the drinks had taken hold and the inhibitions were very much gone. The magnetism that this man held for her became a tremendous challenge that she wanted to meet as a woman.

She stood. He took her in his arms and their lips met. It began gently and ended in a brutal grinding together of mouths and a desperate straining of bodies, one against the other, until he roughly held her away.

"Do you believe me now?" he asked huskily.

She was too shaken to answer. Whatever had happened between them before was transcended at this moment. She remembered his words—"If that adds up to love, then I love you." And he had said, "You're my woman." The words echoed through her consciousness. What other destiny could there be for a woman than to be a woman for a man? Suddenly she ached for his arms and hands. All her inhibitions, reservations and caution were blindly swept aside in sudden desire.

"Yes," she whispered. "Oh, yes …"

He picked her up and carried her to a bed and put her down. He left her for a few moments and turned out all lights except for the soft glow of one shaded lamp.

She waited with eyes closed, trying not to think, not wanting to reason or decide—just to wait and experience. He bent over her and his lips found a pulse in her throat. His hands were on her.

"I love you," he whispered. "I want you."

Somehow the mechanics of undressing—the unsnappings and unzippings, taking-off and shrugging-out-of—were accomplished smoothly and quickly. She turned and lifted and helped him.

He left her again, but only for seconds. She heard the sounds of his undressing and then he was back with her and she felt his male body against her.

She opened her eyes and looked into his face. "Can I believe you?" she asked. "Please …? I don't want to do this unless I can."

"You can believe me."

"I'm not—I'm not—" She tried to voice her last reticence.

"I know," he said and moved with purpose.

"Please don't if—"

"I do," he said.

He took her. She gasped, and moaned as she retreated for an instant, and then, with an age-old, ritualistic movement, she welcomed him in the complete and encompassing embrace of female reception.

Now she was to learn the fulfillments brought by the mature man of experience, the confident man of knowledge, the dominating man of conquest. Even as she previously had recognized that Ken Nytrack was a man—as Jimmy had been a boy, as Clint was a boy—she recognized again that in this most intimate of relations between man and woman, Ken Nytrack was the man, and not the boy; that he was awakening new, unexplored depths of her womanhood.

A complete dissolution of inhibitions in her response was followed by a complete abandonment that made her lovemaking shameless, pleading and primitive. Once she screamed softly—once she cried out in pure ecstasy—once she moaned as a hurt animal—and finally she whispered softly, "Again, again, again …"

Much later, exhausted and motionless, she let him caress her with a firm hand. She turned her head and looked at him, almost in wonderment. Once she had read a clinical dissertation about women who experienced "multiple orgasms" and she had found it difficult to believe. There had been repeated love-making between Jimmy and her on occasion, but never the multiple climactic moments during one love-making. Only Ken Nytrack had given her this new, almost devastating experience.

"Do you love me?" she asked softly.

"You're my woman," he said.

"That isn't what I asked."

"You're my woman," he said again. "That's answer enough. Go to sleep. There's no need for you to go back to your room."

Too tired to think more about it, and satiated beyond belief, she shut her eyes and almost instantly she was asleep.

They returned to Hollywood the following afternoon.

"I'll pick you up for dinner at about eight," he told her when he left her at her apartment. "I may leave for Rome tomorrow."

After he was gone she took a long, relaxing bath and thought about what had happened. No man, no event, had so completely upset her life as Ken Nytrack had. It hardly seemed possible that in less than forty-eight hours so much could happen in a person's life. It was only the night before last that she had been preparing to go out with Clint to meet Ken Nytrack. But in the fast pace of Nytrack's life, forty-eight hours could equal days or even weeks in the lives of others.

His courtship had been keyed to that pace, yet it had been strangely complete. Whatever had gone into the making of the courtship, she never had been so deeply shaken and changed by another person. Even now, as she thought about their first love-making, she felt weakness and abandonment. Certainly he must love her. Such coming together of a man and a woman could not possibly be so complete without love. Above all else, she was conscious of a deep happiness that Ken Nytrack had brought her.

She was dressed and waiting for him when the telephone rang.

Nytrack's voice was tinged with regret. "We'll have to cancel it, darling," he told her. "Business. I'm leaving for Rome in the morning."

"Oh." Her disappointment was sharp. "But I'll see you, won't I? I mean before you go?"

"I'm afraid not. I'm taking an early jet. But you'll be in Rome with a few weeks, and I'll call you when I get there."

"I could wait up tonight ..."

He laughed softly. "I love you. I wish we could, but I'll be working on budgets and schedules almost until plane time."

"I could come to the airport."

"No. Get a good sleep. You'll get a call this evening from the studio. We're setting up your coaching schedules. You start in the morning."

"But, Ken—"

"Look, baby, I've a room full of conference. I'll call you from Rome." She heard the click at the other end of the line.

"I love you, Ken," she whispered.

Slowly she put down her telephone. Everything was happening too fast. She knew so little about him, and she had entrusted so much of herself to him, and deep down she felt such an odd uneasiness. She tried to shrug off the feeling.

"So here I am—dressed to go out, and hungry," she said aloud.

Impulsively she dialed Sam Berill and was surprised to find him at his apartment.

"Sam, would you like to take me to dinner tonight? I don't mean a big date because I have to get up early. But I'm all dressed up and in the mood. I'll even buy the dinner!"

"Delighted!" he told her. "And I'm sober, too—so you won't have any problems! I'll even buy!"

"Could we go to Dino's?"

"You sound sort of celebrity-ish," he chuckled. "Dino's it is."

An hour later they were ordering in Dino's when Sam stopped speaking in the middle of a sentence.

Kima looked at him curiously and followed the line of his gaze. A small, cold knot seemed to tie itself inside her and then she was certain that she was blushing furiously.

Ken Nytrack and Marianne Thurlow had just come in. The actress possessively clutched one of his arms, and Nytrack was looking down into her face and smiling.

Sam glanced knowingly and nervously at Kima. Evidently he had suspected the canceled date. She met the look and managed a smile.

"Yes, Sam. I had a date with him—he said it was a conference."

"Hell!" Sam said. "Damn it to hell!"

"It isn't your fault, Sam. It happens all the time in this town. Besides, maybe it *is* business—only I know it isn't."

"Do you want to leave?"

Now Ken and Marianne saw Kima. Marianne smiled thinly and seemed to move a little closer to Nytrack. She deliberately changed their course to pass the table.

"Kello, Kiva—or is it Kima?" she purred.

Kima smiled, feeling as if her lips were frozen. She looked beyond Marianne into Ken's face. He was watching the small tableau with obvious amusement.

"Hello, Kima," he said. "A slight change in plans."

"I gather that," Kima said quietly.

Marianne casually said, "I suppose we'll see you in Rome. Ken and I leave on the morning jet—right after breakfast."

Kima felt the blush again and fought desperately to control it. Marianne's insinuation was obvious. Ken smilingly urged the actress on past the table with a hand at her elbow. He looked down at Kima.

"Did the studio get you?" he asked.

"No. I asked Sam to have dinner with me when you—"

Nytrack nodded indifferently. "You'd better call the studio. Ask for Carl Manac. He's working out your schedule tonight— he'll tell you where to report in the morning." He nodded curtly, ignoring Sam, and went on with Marianne. Kima fought to hold back tears.

"Baby," Sam said. "Look, don't let it—"

She quickly wiped away the tears and smiled. "Oh, Sam— I'm sorry. I didn't introduce you, and they're people you should know. I mean, now that I'm going to do a picture for him and—"

"It's all right," Sam smiled. "I understand."

"Sam—you're awfully sweet. That's old-fashioned, but you are! "

"Sure," Sam grinned. "Still want to order—or leave?"

"Would it be all right if we—?"

"I know a good place to get hamburgers."

"Yes, Sam, hamburgers—let's get out of here."

CHAPTER SEVEN

THE NEXT TWO WEEKS were to be the most difficult that she ever experienced. Ken Nytrack's aides were tyrants. The voice coach, dramatic coach and other experts drove her unmercifully. Clothes were designed for her. Her hair was styled. Makeup experts worked with her. Each seemed to know exactly what Ken Nytrack wanted, and each apparently considered Kima to be a property, a body to be molded, a voice to be trained, a mind to be disciplined.

At night she came home to her apartment and sometimes fell into bed and slept without eating, exhausted and whimpering in her fatigue.

Despite his promise to call, she heard nothing from Ken Nytrack, but Milo Ginz told her that she would soon fly to Rome for some necessary location shots.

"Aren't they shooting all the picture there?" she asked.

"Not the part written around Los Angeles. They want to do location shots here, too."

"Milo, I'm so tired. I'll look terrible."

"You'll look thin and ready. You got a dramatic, thin look. He knows what he's doing. Besides, you like what you're learning, no?"

"Of course! What girl wouldn't?"

"You're asking me that, darling? Lots of girls would rather get there in bed. You're making it the hard-work, talent way. You'll do okay. Real good."

"I hope so, Milo. But I'm so—so *damned* tired!"

"Maybe that's good, too. This way you got no time for anything but work. You got to remember how it is between you and Ken."

Kima looked at him and thought about his words. She thought back over the relatively few days since she had met Ken Nytrack, and what had happened to her during those days. An odd and unexpected fear assailed her.

"Milo," she said, "Milo, how *is* it between Ken and me? You tell me—suddenly I don't know."

"You could cut my throat for what I say. How can I let my neck be ready for cutting like this? I ask you?"

"You haven't answered me, Milo."

"I told you once. He can be a son-of-a-bitch."

By the end of those two weeks the first stories about Kima's role in *Ground Rules* appeared in trade papers. A brash young man named Cliff Cation made his appearance the day after Nytrack left for Rome and explained that he handled press relations for Nytrack. He had been instructed to begin a build-up for her.

Even as he was introducing himself—he found her at the studio of her voice coach—a call came from Milo for Kima.

"There's a young man named Cation who'll see you," the agent said. "He handles publicity for Nytrack. You talk with him. It's okay."

"He's here now," she said. "What about Sam?"

"Nytrack left word he'd just as soon Sam doesn't work on this."

"But Sam's my friend, Milo! I can't do this to him."

"Baby, this is *business*. Right now you better do what Cation says. It's expedient, yes? It'll be all right. I, Milo Ginz, promise you someday we make this up to Sam."

Reluctantly she agreed.

She didn't like Cation. He was an energetic, intense young man. His clothing looked impeccably Ivy League. He wore his hair short, and he displayed the usual dark-rimmed glasses. His attitude betrayed a continual impatience with everyone, and a disdain for anyone not his superior. He was smart, and he knew it.

He put Kima through a small ordeal of interviews with reporters from fan magazines, with columnists, and sessions with photographers.

"Christ, that name!" he said impatiently.

"What's wrong with it?" Kima angrily demanded.

"Kima looks like Kim. Kim relates to Novak. You're not Novak."

"I'm not Kipling's Kim, either. I'm Kima. And what's Kima got to do with Novak?"

"Psychological association. Brand image," he said mockingly.

"So you took a few hours of psych. Don't parade it. I did, too."

"I forgot that you went to college, baby," he smiled. "Let's not fight. I have to create you into something. That sounds better than saying that I have to make you—although I'd like that, too."

"I don't like you."

He shrugged. "So? I'm just doing a job. Now—they're working up layouts for *Stars in Your Eyes*, the fan mag. I'll need some of your time tomorrow. Maybe I can break something soon with Louella or Army Archer. Now, your image—"

He interrupted himself to light a cigarette.

"Your image—Ken says under no circumstances do we make you a homebody-type girl," he continued. "That's passé. We give you a good theatrical background. And we make you clean and healthy. Nothing cheap about you. Real smart career girl. Serious. Ken found you, recognized your talent, brings you to the world in the most important vehicle filmed in the last ten years—*Ground Rules*, the sophisticated, frank, startling story of the rules of mating and marriage as played today in the smart International Set."

Kima listened without comment. He sounded a little like Sam.

"No love interests," he concluded. "Ken spelled that out. No time for men right now. All career until you find just the man you want. A man who can measure up to your own stature. That's a good line."

"Look, Mr. Cation—"

"Cliff, baby."

"*Mr. Cation*—can't we hurry this? I still have a busy schedule."

"Sure, sure! One more thing—you're moving to the Studio Club."

"The Studio Club? But that's a residence for girls only!"

"As they say, 'a supervised residence for young Hollywood actresses.' We think the image it'll create by your living there will—"

"No."

"Orders, baby," Cation said quietly.

"No. I've lived alone in rooms and apartments for too long to give up what I consider to be my adult, mature—"

"Okay, okay! You'll be in Rome soon. Take it up then with Ken."

"No Studio Club."

"And remember—no dates. Men, that is."

"No *love* interest, maybe," she said. "But I have friends who—"

"Ken says no dates. Your name's not to be associated with *any* man's right now. Not while we're making the picture.

Maybe he has ideas about something over there, studio inspired. Maybe you and Glasgow."

Kima sighed. There was no point in being angry with this brash, energetic young man. He was only doing his job.

"All right," Kima said. "Make me into an image. Make a nun of me. A recluse, an old maid, a career woman. Anything you need. Only get it over with. I have so many things to do—I'm so *tired*."

"Okay, okay," Cation smiled placatingly. "I'll bunch the interviews. We'll take our own stills for the mag layouts. We want sex—plenty of sex—but no cheap leg art. You're above that—the smart, sophisticated, career gal with talent who's going places. You're stacked. But you're not displaying it for creeps who need it for kicks—only for normal creeps who maybe are sick of their wives and like to look."

"Oh, shut up, Cation. You bore me. Do your work and get done."

He shook his head sadly. "Don't treat me like that, Kima. I might start to *like* you for it."

Several evenings later, shortly after she had arrived home after a hard day, Sam called upon her. He had been drinking.

"I shouldn't let you in, Sam," she told him. "I'm tired and I should go to bed."

"I just want to talk a little while, Kima."

She went to her kitchen and mixed drinks for them. She had just come from a shower and wore only a terrycloth robe and slippers, but she felt no nervousness with him. Although he had intimated that he would have liked more than a platonic friendship, she felt a strange security with him.

He stretched long legs and studied the unpolished toes of the loafers he wore. "Know something?" he said. "This may sound square as a Harvey, but I want to tell you. I mean, the way I feel about you. If I were the marrying, eligible kind, and you could look at me with more than tolerance for a lush in your eyes, I'd be tempted to ask you to be Mrs. Sam Berill. And I haven't felt that way about a girl since—well, for a long time. So don't laugh, and just remember what I said and sit there and be beautiful. I like to just look at you."

She looked at him and felt her own tenderness showing in her eyes. If he had been a little more of a lush, a little less of a man, and a little more wistful, she might have pitied him. Love him, she never could. But she would always feel tenderness toward him.

"Sam—I don't know what to say...."

"Don't say anything. I just wanted to tell you. No—don't move. I'll refill the drinks."

She lit a cigarette while he was busy in the kitchen and wondered how he really felt about being taken off the job of helping her. He probably was hurt.

He returned with drinks and slouched again in the chair. He contemplated the toes of his loafers again and said, "Don't get sore, but I've got to ask you something."

"I won't get sore."

"What's really between you and Ken Nytrack?"

"That's a pretty personal-type question, Sam."

"I know. But I figure if I love you I can be personally interested in what happens to you—and you might understand that."

"I might," she admitted. "Why do you ask?"

"Has Milo said anything about Nytrack?"

She took a short swallow of her drink and nodded. "Yes."

"Was he honest with you?"

"That's an unfair question," she smiled. "How would I know? I *think* he was honest about what he thought."

"Can you tell me? Or do you want to?"

"He said Ken can be a son-of-a-bitch. That's an exact quote."

Sam finished his second drink and again put down the glass. "Then you know," he said. "I just wanted to be sure."

"You're really concerned about me, aren't you, Sam!"

"I love you, Kima. I may never tell you that again. Just wanted to say it right and proper once. And I *am* concerned. Please watch things."

"With Ken?"

"And with Marianne. She isn't happy about things."

"You mean about me?"

He nodded gravely. "I heard from a good source that she's out to make it rough for you."

"Should I be worried about her, Sam?"

He gave her a small, amused smile. "Well, as Milo says, Ken's a son-of-a-bitch. And Marianne—well, she's just plain bitch. You're damned right you should be worried, Kima. Hasn't Milo mentioned it?"

"He's been out of town."

Sam got up to leave. Kima went to the door with him. Impulsively she stood on tiptoes and kissed him. His arms tightened about her and he held her closely and then pushed her away.

"This kid likes candy," he said. "Don't tempt him with samples, baby!"

"Thanks for coming—for telling me—and for feeling as you do about me, Sam. I'm sorry I don't—I mean, I like you and—"

"Don't try, Kima. I'm a big boy. Just remember what I told you. Watch the son-of-a-bitch and the bitch. They can cause you trouble."

"Sam, one question. Do you know Bill Rold? I met him in Vegas."

"I know him. Mostly by reputation."

"And?"

"He's very hep—very smooth—very smart. A guy more noted for what people *don't* know about him than what they *do*. You read that?"

"I think so."

He hesitated, looking at her oddly. "Anything you want to tell me?"

"No. Thanks again for everything."

"Sure. And good luck. Any time you need a shoulder to cry on or a fast gun for a showdown, call me, huh?" He smiled.

"I'll remember that, Sam."

He left and she closed the door after him. Her telephone was ringing. She answered the call and Cliff Cation said, "Start packing, baby. They want you in Rome. We've reservations on tonight's jet."

She digested the words, almost with shock. "But I'm not ready!" she protested.

"As ready as you'll ever be. Don't worry about taking much. Everything you'll need is over there. I'll pick you up in two hours."

The telephone clicked as he hung up. She stared at the dead instrument. Suddenly she was very frightened, and she wasn't certain why.

CHAPTER EIGHT

K EN NYTRACK did not meet the jet in Rome. Kima might have been more disappointed if she had not been almost in a daze from fatigue, the sudden and rather long plane trip, the effort to sleep aloft, the sporadic outbursts of conversation from Cliff Cation, and the simple excitement of going to Europe and Rome.

In a comparatively few hours Kima was installed in a hotel, given a few glimpses of the great Italian city, and accosted by a tireless cortege of studio personnel engaged with the task of preparing her for her filming, which was to begin the day after she arrived.

Finally—and unexpectedly, at about the dinner hour—Ken appeared. He looked tan, fit and a little tired. He came into Kima's small hotel suite while she was having a lastmoment fitting for some wardrobe changes. She put on a robe over her slip and went to him with outstretched hands. She wondered if he would kiss her in the presence of two wardrobe people from the studio. Then she noticed the tall, blond man standing in the doorway behind Ken.

"Kima!" Nytrack smiled warmly. He took her hands and there was to be no kiss. She sensed that at once. "You look wonderful!" he said. He motioned toward the blond man. "You know Rick Glasgow?"

She had recognized the male star immediately, but she never had met him. Nytrack quickly finished the introduction. Glasgow smiled pleasantly. "Good flight?" he asked Kima.

"Yes," she smiled. The wardrobe workers were ready to leave. Nytrack already was on a telephone ordering drinks. He put down the instrument and wearily sat in a convenient chair, motioning Glasgow to another. "It's been a day," he said to Kima. He glanced at Glasgow. "Ask Rick! He did most of the work."

Glasgow smiled deprecatingly. "You did the heavy work, Ken. Directing is as tough a job as a man can inherit."

Ken chuckled. "Not every star would admit that," he said.

"Anyone who knows the business admits it," Glasgow said. "Smart people check the director of a picture to know its worth."

"Our friend Rick is heading that way himself." Nytrack smiled at Kima. "He wants to direct eventually. He'll do all right. Not too many do. And God help the ones who can't, but think they can and become independent producers without sense enough to hire a competent director and listen to him. Because a star is a great actor doesn't mean that he can produce and direct a show himself and come out with anything worth seeing."

"I agree," Glasgow said quietly. "My idea of being an independent, at this stage of the game, would be to produce a show, star in it, but hire you, or Billy Wilder, Stevens, Wyler, Kazan, Fellini or one of the other top names to direct it."

Ken looked at the actor with calculating eyes. "You're a smart man, Rick," he said. "You couldn't hire me. I'll produce *and* direct my *own* shows. I'll do all the hiring. But someday you'll be rough competition, and I'll remember how much you've learned by watching the rest of us."

"That's sort of a left-handed compliment," Glasgow smiled. He looked at Kima. "Truly, I'm delighted to meet you and I'm looking forward to working with you."

"Thank you." Kima smiled. She was pleased to meet the English actor, and seeing him now off screen she realized that he must be well into his forties. Possibly this was why he was becoming interested in directing.

"You'll meet Marc Ozzino tomorrow," Ken told her. "He's in the supporting role to Rick. He's having language trouble, but he's coming along."

She remembered seeing the young Sicilian actor in several Italian pictures. This was his first major English-speaking role.

Curiously she wondered if any mention would be made of Marianne. She certainly was not going to ask about the red-headed actress, but she was curious to know how she was getting along in the picture—and, more important, what was happening between the actress and Ken Nytrack.

Drinks arrived and the two men savored theirs with the obvious enjoyment of a first drink after a hard day of work.

"We're taking you out to dinner," Ken told her. "And maybe an hour or two of Via Veneto—the avenue—and some of the clubs. We'll let the *paparazzi* get a few shots at you."

"The photographers? *La Dolce Vita?*" she smiled.

Glasgow nodded. "They say that Fellini coined the name for them when he was directing *La Dolce Vita*—comparing them with buzzing, darting, stinging insects. They're truly a nuisance sometimes."

"Do they really run in packs?"

"Yes," Glasgow said. "With cameras and flashguns ready. And as long as news services, magazines and newspapers will buy their pictures, the *paparazzi* are in business."

"As a matter of fact," Ken added, "if the celebrities aren't doing enough to make good news, the *paparazzi* may create something. The night they got shots of Anita at Howard's party, they sneaked in their own belly dancer for added excitement."

Glasgow glanced at Ken Nytrack. "Are we meeting Marianne, as usual?"

Nytrack nodded. "I want to talk about tomorrow's shooting. Dinner's the best place."

He finished his drink. "Let's get on with it. Kima, you'd better dress."

For a moment she was almost panic-striken. She wasn't certain what she should wear. "I'll be right back," she said. She went into the bedroom of the suite. A maid, assigned to her from the hotel through the studio, had solved her problem. A frock was waiting. The maid smiled. "Thees one?" she asked. "It will be nice, no?" She seemed to sense Kima's uncertainty.

"We're going to dinner—in Via Veneto, I assume," she said. "That's where they go, isn't it?"

"It ees like Hollywood Streep, no?" The woman smiled in just the correct amount of subservient friendliness.

"That's what I've heard," Kima said. With the aid of the maid she quickly dressed and went out to rejoin the men. Nytrack was at the telephone discussing something about the picture, the conversation generously sprinkled with technical terms.

The tall Englishman still was working on his drink and stood near a window looking down into the street. He turned when Kima entered the room and gave her a quick, masculine look of appraisal. His smile signified his approval.

"Hungry?" he asked.

"I haven't eaten all day. There seems to be so much to do."

"I know," he said. He left the window and joined Kima where she sat on a couch. Nytrack still was busy at the telephone.

"How is the picture going?" Kima asked, wondering if it was the right thing to say.

"Excellent. I enjoy working with Marianne. You know her, of course?"

"Yes, but not too well."

"She's a talented woman. I don't wonder that Ken values her so very highly."

"Yes, he does, doesn't he?" Kima said.

Glasgow looked at her, almost sharply, as if he had detected a pique in Kima's voice. He didn't pursue the subject further.

"Your first time in Rome?" he asked.

"My first time out of the United States," Kima admitted.

"You'll like it. But it may not be as different as you anticipated. It seems that the whole world is becoming rather regimented. You'll see the same Hollywood faces on Via Veneto. The music will sound the same as in Hollywood—or New York—or Paris— or Tokyo. It's pretty much the same everywhere. Everything is. Except in the old things that may remain. And in Rome you still find a patina and glory of history."

Nytrack finished his telephone conversation. He came over to the couch and took Kima's hand. She felt the pressure of his fingers. It was the first truly personal gesture that he had given her since her arrival.

"It's good to see you, Kima," he smiled. "Ready?"

"Yes. Mr. Glasgow and I have been talking about—"

" 'Rick,' " the actor interrupted. " 'Mr. Glasgow' is much too formal, Kima. I've been preparing her a little for Rome," he added to Ken.

"Good. Now let's get on with it. We'll see how well Rome and those damned *paparazzi* are prepared for *her*. Lovely, isn't she, Rick?"

"Lovely," Glasgow said. "I'm glad we'll be working together."

As they left the room it was Rick Glasgow's hand gently upon her elbow, rather than Ken Nytrack's. Kima felt a small sickness of disappointment. She had expected Ken to be truly happy to see her, to reflect what he had said to her weeks before, and the relationship she had assumed was between them.

Any exuberance of being with her again, of seeing her again, of even touching her hand again, seemed to be lacking—or deliberately covered by his attitude of simple friendliness. She might have been any actress in his employ, but certainly not the girl he had held so rapturously in his arms less than a month ago in a Las Vegas hotel bed.

Was his indifference due to the presence of another man? Because they were not alone? Or was it something else?

She wished that she could be alone with him. She felt an urgent need to know exactly how things stood between them. Most of all, she felt a great need to quiet the restless uneasiness she had felt for weeks.

The *paparazzi* were clustered at the entrance of the café on Via Veneto where they went to eat. Most of the photographers apparently recognized Nytrack and the English actor, and they looked inquisitively at Kima. A few lifted cameras and took pictures. One asked who she was and Ken smiled and told them.

"Kima Shannon?" the inquirer persisted. "So, who is Kima Shannon?"

"She'll be in *Ground Rules,*" Nytrack said crisply and ushered his guests inside.

Almost before they had settled into their chairs Marianne joined them. Her dress was cut daringly low, even for Continental fashions. She smiled her small, catlike smile at Kima.

"*Kiva!*" she smiled. "How nice!"

"It's *Kima*," Ken said, the familiar look of amusement coming again to his eyes. "And you're smiling like a cat again, baby."

Marianne laughed gaily and made a small moue at him. She turned to Rick Glasgow. "You were wonderful today, Rick," she said. "I do hope Kiva—I mean Kima—will work out well with you in the scenes tomorrow. But then, you make *any-one* look good, Rick. And you're such a *charitable* English gentleman!"

Ken Nytrack openly laughed. "All right, Marianne. Knock it off. You've made your point. Kima has enough to do without fending off your claws!" He seemed genuinely amused by Marianne's behavior.

Kima's anger was close to the breaking point. She was about to answer the redheaded actress with a scathing remark when Rick Glasgow caught her eye with a warning look. She repressed the retort and smiled instead. "I'm anxious to start work," she said.

Marianne turned her full attention to Ken, closing the other two out of the conversation:

"Ken, dear, can we talk a little about the soliloquy scene when I'm alone on the beach?"

"We won't shoot that for two or three days. We can talk about it later."

"No. It's so important to the picture. I want to be thinking about it now—I want to be able to *feel* it when I get into it."

Rick and Kima exchanged glances. Marianne was making an obvious attempt to absorb Ken's full attention, and to ignore Kima and Rick. Kima felt anger rise again and she caught herself almost biting her lips. Rick Glasgow smiled at her.

"This place is famous, in its own way," he told her. "You'll probably see more world-famous—or infamous—people here in a shorter time than almost anywhere. At least, you'll see more scandal in the making."

"Is Rome really as—well, *bad* as they say? I mean the picture colony?"

"It's as they say Hollywood was thirty years ago. Young people flock here from all over the world—trying to look like

Brando, Bardot, Cardinale, Marianne, the others. And there's the professional Hollywood crowd that has virtually moved here. Mingling with the picture crowd are some of what's left of Continental nobility, big business tycoons, celebrities from other arts. Café Carpano is a melting pot in its own right when it comes to names, people and personalities."

Across the table Ken talked seriously with Marianne, and—oddly enough, Kima thought—Marianne was listening with close attention. Abruptly Kima realized that Marianne was much more than a woman, or—as Sam had suggested—a typical bitch. She was a good actress who paid concentrated attention to her work. It was obvious in the way in which she was listening to Ken's instructions now. She was a capable, beautiful and dangerous woman.

It was Marianne who brought an end to the dinner.

"It's getting late," she suddenly announced. "And tomorrow will be a difficult one on the set—for all of us. Ken, will you take me home now?"

For a fraction of a moment he looked at her with the small, familiar expression of amusement that Kima was beginning to recognize. He locked eyes with Marianne, as if to say, "I know what you're doing." Then he nodded and looked at Kima and Glasgow.

"She's right," he said. "We all need some rest. You have a morning call, Kima—although over here most companies are devoted to the one-in-the-afternoon-to-eight-or-nine-in-the-evening schedule. I still work the Hollywood way."

Almost tensely, Kima looked at him. Was this the way her first night in Rome was to end? Ken saw the question in her eyes and shrugged a little, almost apologetically.

"Actually it still is fairly early," he said. "I know Marianne is tired and I'm beat. But there's no reason why you two shouldn't look around a while. Rick, would you mind taking Kima back to the hotel? You might show her a little of the street, and possibly a fast spin through the city in that sports car of yours."

"Delighted," Rick said.

"But skip the fountain bit, darling," Marianne smiled sweetly at Kima. "It won't work any more."

Kima looked at her, puzzled. "I don't know what you—"

"But of course you know!" Marianne interrupted. "How all the ambitious young starlets took to midnight bathing in the 'beautiful fountains of Rome' to attract attention—and the *paparazzi!* And it actually worked for some, if they wore little enough, got wet enough and showed enough."

"If you think I'd—" Kima started to say angrily.

"But now," Marianne interrupted again, flaunting her smile, "they have policemen stationed at the fountains to stop you. So don't waste your time. On second thought, you wouldn't have much to show, anyhow." She looked into Rick's face and said, "See you tomorrow, darling." She turned to Ken and put a possessive hand on an arm, in her familiar gesture. "Shall we go, dear?"

Ken eyed her with an arched eyebrow, and then with a small shrug he laughed. He leaned forward and kissed Kima lightly on the cheek.

"Sleep well, baby," he said. "Tomorrow we work." To Glasgow he said, "Take good care of her—and to bed fairly early? Please? We're making a picture, you know."

"Early to bed," Rick said. "We'll float around a little to give Kima a look, but I promise to have her in bed by midnight."

"Literally?" Marianne asked brightly.

"You're picking up some of that flaunted Roman decadence," Glasgow smiled at her. "Good night, angel."

He remained standing until they left, and then sat down and thoughtfully looked across the table at Kima. Silently she stared down at the table, not even attempting to analyze her own feelings of anger, hurt and disappointment.

"Well?" Rick finally said.

Kima looked up and saw the friendliness in his eyes. She instinctively liked this man who had made a fine career on the stage and screen, mostly in England. With the increasing popularity of foreign films, he had gained a large following of fans in the United States.

"I think I'd like a good, strong drink," she said. "Maybe two."

"No more," he smiled. "We won't let it become one of those nights. Two strong drinks. Then I'll show you around a little, deliver you safely to your hotel, and you'll still have time for a good sleep before your very important day tomorrow."

She nodded, wondering how much he knew about Ken and her. She suspected that he knew quite a bit, or at least guessed it.

Meanwhile, if ever a woman had been "put down," outmaneuvered, ignored by a man who should have desired her, she was that woman. It made her angry. So angry that it might just be possible that she would consider inviting this nice Englishman to share her bed tonight. While Ken Nytrack was enjoying his redheaded star, she—Kima Shannon—could be retaliating in like manner! It would serve him right! It would be just payment! It would—

Abruptly she quietly laughed at herself. She knew that she never could do such a thing for such a reason.

"Something funny?" Glasgow asked pleasantly.

"Just philosophical. I was just thinking that you can't build self-respect by tearing it down." She smiled at him. "Now let's have our two strong drinks!"

"Your philosophy of the moment is a little ambiguous," he said. "But I think I know what you mean. And Kima—"

"Yes?"

"You have a wonderful smile. Don't ever lose it!"

CHAPTER NINE

BY AFTERNOON of the following day Kima was finding it more difficult every moment to show the smile that Rick Glasgow had admired.

True to his promise, he had shown her some of the excitement along the broad Via Veneto and the night spots, the floor shows, the people. He had driven her in a fast, low Italian sports car through narrow, ancient streets and out along modern concourses.

For a few hours she had tasted Rome at night, and she had found it to be exciting and charming with Rick Glasgow as a guide. It had been almost one o'clock in the morning when they finally had returned to her hotel, and he had left her at the door, reminding her of her early call.

In the morning a studio car had picked her up, whisked her through surprisingly active Italian traffic to a studio. That had been hours ago. Now beneath lights, before cameras, in the presence of strange surroundings, among people she really didn't know, and under the pressure that Ken Nytrack could generate, she was near to tears—or screams.

All had gone well through some rather unimportant scenes, but now in Kima's first important scene everything seemed to go wrong.

The scene was not particularly complex and Kima knew that she should easily handle it with her training and experience. But it wasn't working out that way.

In the script, a girl named Alicia—played by Kima—was to discover that her fiancé was involved with another woman, and this was the scene in which Alicia vented her anger upon the man, played by Marc Ozzino, the young Sicilian actor.

After considerable rehearsal, the first take began fairly well until Nytrack interrupted the action.

"Kima—*anger!* I want *anger* in this scene. Let's try it again."

Kima and Ozzino took their places again. Kima concentrated upon her lines as they waited briefly. Nytrack started the action.

Kima read her lines: *"I know ... I know what has happened."*

Ozzino took her into his arms: *"But, darling ... it doesn't mean anything."*

Firmly Kima pushed him away from her: *"No ... we're finished—"*

"Cut! " Nytrack snapped the order.

The action stopped and the people on the set faced him. He looked at Kima, obviously trying to make his smile patient.

"Kima," he said. "You're too gentle. You don't just quietly and calmly remove his arms from around you. *Break out. Be assertive.*"

"But wouldn't a woman be more coldly decisive?" Kima asked defensively.

"Not this woman. And, Kima—let me do the interpreting? I think it will work out better."

Kima felt the rebuff in his voice and smarted under it. She set her lips, almost defiantly.

"All right," she conceded. "With assertion."

They began the scene again.

Kima: *"I know ... I know what has happened—"*

Nytrack interrupted again. "Hold it. Look ... let's rehearse this again. Carefully. Kima, your emphasis is not on *happened.* It's on *know*. We've already gone over this several times. You're back to accenting *happened.*"

Kima listened sullenly. Nytrack was right. In rehearsal he carefully had coached her with the line, and now she had blown it. She was becoming tired and nervous.

"I'm sorry," she said. "I don't need to rehearse it again. "I'll remember."

"Okay," Nytrack said wearily. "Let's try again. It's a take."

They began the scene again. Marc Ozzino took Kima into his arms. She pushed him away. "*No ...*" She remembered Nytrack's instructions. Her voice chilled. Abruptly she couldn't remember the line. She faltered and stared at Ozzino in alarm.

"Cut!" Nytrack interrupted again. "Kima—*please!*"

"I'm sorry," Kima said, angry with herself. "All right—I'm *sorry.*"

"Let's try it again," Nytrack said. He was not smiling.

They took their places, Kima fiercely repeating her lines to herself, determined to give a perfect performance. She heard Nytrack's command to start the action. She stared at Ozzino and realized that she was speaking her lines and going through the action, but she was working automatically, lifelessly, and she couldn't do anything about it. It was as if she were marching and suddenly got out of step and could not get back in step with others.

"No! No! *No!*" Nytrack cried, his voice cracking like a whip. He stopped the action again. Marc Ozzino looked at the director with an expression as close to disgust as he would allow himself with an employer. Nytrack ignored him and directed his full attention to Kima.

"Kima," he said softly—too softly. "Kima—have you the slightest idea what you are supposed to be doing? Do you even have an inkling of the person you are portraying? Do you even know that you are enacting a role—a part—a characterization? "

Kima glared at him. Her head ached violently. She was almost nauseated from the work, the heat, the strain. She didn't know how she could possibly look like a woman—even a human being—after the ordeal of frustrating hours she already had experienced.

"I'm beginning not to give a damn who, what, or why I'm in this damned picture," she said in a low, intense voice. "I'm getting sick of it—of this Sicilian I'm trying to work with—and most of all of you, Ken Nytrack. And if that buys me a return jet ticket to California, that's fine with me."

Her angry explosion brought an instant quiet to the set. Even the Italian workers who might not understand English could understand the anger in this woman's voice. They looked upon her not without admiration.

To one side of the set, sitting out of the lights where she had been quietly watching, Marianne laughed softly.

"Temperament!" she said. "My, my!"

"And *you*—" Kima said, turning toward Marianne—"you—"

Nytrack interrupted sharply. "All right. We'll do it again. From the start."

Marianne smiled at Kima. "Keep trying, Kiva—I mean Kima. You'll—"

"*Shut up!*" Nytrack abruptly snapped at the redheaded actress. "Get off the set, Marianne. You're through for the day. We've work to do here, and you're not helping things."

"Don't you—!" Marianne was standing, eyes flashing as she stared at Nytrack.

"Don't push it," Nytrack said quietly. "Remember—don't push it, Marianne. Just leave quietly so we can forget this."

The actress was motionless for a moment, obviously trying to control another impending outburst. Finally she managed to laugh again. "Very well," she said. "Tonight—as usual?"

He nodded impatiently. "Yes." Already he was turning back to Kima and the male actor. The cameramen and assistants watched and waited.

"Now you listen to me," Nytrack said to Kima, advanc-upon her. "And you listen good. We're making a picture. A good picture. I won't stand for anything in it that isn't good. I demand the best. I demand *perfection*. And you're going to give it to me for this scene—and every scene you do for me."

Kima remained motionless, glaring at him in undiminished anger.

Nytrack held up the script and pointed to it. "Look at it!" he cried. "*Read* it! Read the *words!* Read the *meaning!* Do you see what it says? I'll read it to you: *Alicia wrenches herself out of Sabin's arms* ... Alicia," Nytrack barked. "That's you, Kima—remember? *You* are *Alicia*. And Marc is Sabin. Am I being too elementary?"

She stared at him in her blazing anger. They had gone over the scene at least twenty times. She knew every word of the script; the directions, the words, the plot, the meanings, the inflections—all of it. Nytrack was carrying sarcasm to a crude point of insult.

"Now," Nytrack said in a biting voice, "you—as Alicia—have just discovered that your fiancé, Sabin, has been sleeping with another woman. He tries to take you in his arms. He thinks he can sweet-talk you out of your anger. But you're not having any of it. Is that clear?"

"Yes, that's clear, Mr. Nytrack," Kima said icily.

"So you tell him off. *But you are acting a role in* Ground Rules—do *you understand that?* You are Alicia, a member of the International Set. You are supposed to have education, background, breeding, sophistication, smartness, smoothness. Is that clear?"

"Perfectly."

"Then don't read your lines like a cheap, two-bit taxi dancer out of Dreamland down on skid row!"

"You go to hell, Mr. Nytrack! You take your damned job and your picture and your redheaded bitch and go to hell!"

"Shut up. You're working for me. You're here to do a job. Right now. Is that clear? Right now! All right—action. Get those cameras rolling. Start your scene. You, Marc—grab her, start your lines."

Automatically, and surprised, the young actor put his arms around Kima and nervously began to read his lines—more realistically than he realized.

Just as automatically Kima responded. Her anger was overflowing in a torrent of vindictiveness against Nytrack, but now the lines from the scene exactly fitted her feelings.

She tore herself out of the actor's arms, as the script demanded. The words from the scene came automatically. *"No!"* Her voice was husky with true anger. *"No—we're finished. Completely. I won't be cheapened this way. Not by her—not by you!"*

There were more lines and she swept through them in a rage, wanting to be done, to turn her back upon Ken Nytrack, to walk off the set and out of the studio and away from all of it.

"Okay, okay ... cut!" Nytrack was saying. His voice no longer was angry nor sarcastic. He sounded calm and weary.

Lights faded out and cameramen relaxed. Assistants became active.

"That's all for today," Nytrack announced. He looked at the couple on the set with his smile of amusement. The young Sicilian nervously lit a cigarette.

"All right?" he asked. "All right, Mr. Nytrack?"

"Fine. You were fine in almost every take. It was Kima—until this last one."

"I mean it," Kima said, her anger still blazing. "You can take—"

"Kima, Kima," Nytrack said gently. "Calm down. Cool off. You were great in that last take. Really great. You're an actress—once you're aroused. Eventually you'll learn how to do it without an outside stimulus. But it's there. It's really there."

"I'm going back to the hotel."

"Certainly. I'll drive you myself."

"Don't bother. I have to get this makeup off and I'd rather a studio car took me." Her voice was unyielding.

"As you wish," Nytrack smiled. "Prehaps I'll see you later tonight." He turned and left the two.

Marc Ozzino looked at Kima.

"You were very good," he said in his precise English. "Very good in that last take. Nytrack, he is right. You are an actress. Perhaps I could drive you back to the hotel?"

Kima managed a smile for him. He was a nice young man, but she didn't want to become involved with him, even to the extent of a ride to the hotel. Right now she wanted to nurse and enjoy her anger. She only wished that Marianne were there. She might even manage to sink her fingers into the actress' red hair! Maybe she could *truly* act like a dancer from Dreamland!

It was an hour before she finally calmed herself. By the time she arrived at her hotel suite she was ready for tears. Reaction had set in and she was almost physically ill with it.

She barely had closed the door when a telephone rang.

"I hear that you had a bad day," Rick Glasgow said. "But Ken says you finally turned in a real performance. Congratulations."

"I don't think I deserve congratulations," she said bitterly. "I was working from anger."

"Sometimes the best fuel is anger. How about dinner with me?"

"Alone?"

"If you mean, will it be another like last night—with Ken and Marianne—it's no. They're going to a little gathering put together by a count who wants to get a job as an extra. It's all the fad these days—members of the nobility have decided that it's amusing and smart to work as extras. So I thought I could show you some more of Rome, see that you eat a good dinner, and get you home reasonably early again."

"Thanks, Rick," Kima said, angry again to learn that Ken never had intended to see her this night. At the moment she actively hated him for the whole day, the picture, the role and everything that he had done to her life.

"In an hour?" Glasgow asked.

"In an hour. And, Rick—maybe *three* strong drinks tonight? I really need them."

"Early call in the morning?"

"No. Not until afternoon."

"In that case, not only three, but possibly four—five—or more, if you want them!" he laughed.

Rick Glasgow took full charge of the evening with the enthusiasm of the experienced habitant showing off his city to a visitor. He made certain that she saw all there was to see in the three-block stretch of Via Veneto that extends from the Aurelian Wall to the U.S. Embassy.

Here the *paparazzi* were especially busy. By merely observing their activities it was possible to spot the celebrities.

He took her to the Café de Paris, where she was reminded of *La Dolce Vita*. They tarried at the Hotel Excelsior, where the coming and going of international stars reminded her of a big premiere night in Hollywood.

"It's a favorite place," Rick explained. "Brando, Clift, Loren, Rossellini, Gardner …"

He took her to places where homosexuality was the accent, and to others where he identified Italian beauties as high-priced call girls. He pointed out royalty—a countess who suffered from nymphomania, a count who specialized in sadism, and another who obviously was enamored with the platinum-blond young man who simpered at his side.

"Don't get the idea that royalty is completely decadent," Glasgow smiled. "Far from it—and the virile among the royal blood group are most certainly and completely virile! Ask the woman who marries one—or his mistress!"

"It's fascinating!" Kima admitted, forgetting the unhappiness of the day as the evening wore on, and the drinks came more often than she had anticipated. Rick Glasgow was showing her a good time, and she was most appreciative!

Some of the floor shows reminded her fleetingly of the night she had spent making the Las Vegas rounds with Bill Rold. There seemed to be a casual acceptance of nudity and seminudity everywhere, and the much publicized Italian bosom was amply on display.

Occasionally they stopped at a table and met people, some of whom she recognized, some she did not. The conversation varied from table to table, group to group.

An intense young man pounded a table for emphasis: "Bergman of Sweden … Resnais of France … David Lean, Jack Clayton, Antonioni, Wilder, Preminger—directors, directors, directors! But where in America are the angry *young* men? Where?"

A dark-haired girl, with a young, large and beautifully formed bosom, looked earnestly into the black eyes of the equally dark-haired young man beside her: "But, darling, I cannot come to live with you. My husband would not like it."

A TV star on vacation from Hollywood drank too much and looked bleary-eyed at a Des Moines businessman and his wife. No one knew how they had met, but they were at the same table, all drinking, all intriguingly friendly.

"So I said," the TV star smiled proudly. "I said—pardon me, ma'am—I said, 'Mr. Producer, you just take this series and shove it!' "

A woman with a strange smile and suggestive eyes leaned across a table toward Kima: "But, my dear, how utterly lovely you are. How do you happen to be with Rick? Join me—I could ..."

Rick led her through a maze of quick greetings, introductions, tables, groups, entrances and exits, and past the *paparazzi* with their flashing lights and ready cameras.

Finally they were back at her hotel. He escorted her to her door. She had a strong impulse to ask him in. The drinks, excitement and what she had seen had created a mood for her. Rick had been nice to her. He had been thoughtful. He had been friendly. He could come in.

"A nightcap?" she asked.

He smiled and shook his head. "Not tonight. I still have a fairly early call. Sometime again? It's been fun."

"A lot of fun," she agreed. "Thank you, Rick."

He kissed her lightly and opened her door for her. "Good night."

"Good night, Rick."

She was a little surprised to find lights on in her suite, and she was momentarily startled when she saw a man seated in a comfortable chair by a window.

"A little late, aren't you?" Ken Nytrack asked from the chair.

"How did you get in here?" Kima demanded.

"That's a stupid question, Kima. My company is paying for the suite. This is *my* show. I pay the bills. I get the privileges."

"Not to my privacy!"

He got up from the chair and came toward her. He looked her over with the proprietary look she had seen in his eyes before.

He said, "You're a desirable woman. I'm glad you're here."

"No, Ken. Not this time. You and Marianne are too obvious. And after what you put me through today I can't possibly believe—"

"Believe what?" he interrupted. "That I love you?"

"That's right. I can't believe that you love me."

"You don't know anything about me. With a temperamental star like Marianne in a crucial role I have to keep her happy. Forget her."

Kima shook her head, not entering farther into the room, just standing near the closed door, gazing at Nytrack who had stopped several feet from her. He returned her look with his smile of amusement.

"I have nothing for which to apologize," he said. "Nothing. You're my woman. I told you that in Vegas. I mean it tonight. What has to be done to finish a picture is necessary—any expedience. You've got to understand that about me. Once I start a job, I have to finish it. At any cost. Only it's at no cost to you and me."

"No."

"Today bothers you? How else could I get your emotions aroused to the place where you could do such a beautiful job? That's just a start. You're an actress, Kima. A good one. With work you'll be a great one. If I hurt your feelings, I'm sorry. But I have a small fortune riding on this picture and I need your best—along with Marianne's, Rick's and all the others. Try to understand that, darling."

She listened without betraying her emotions. His voice somehow lulled her anger, and desperately she tried not to believe what he said, yet acknowledging that he might be right. He had a picture to do. He had temperamental persons with whom to work.

He stepped toward her confidently, and before she realized what he was about to do he took her into his arms and his mouth closed upon hers. She felt the familiarity of his hands and tried to fight the excitement they aroused, but knowing that she had been hungry for it.

"Don't," she said. "Don't. I don't want—"

"Stop it. You're my woman. Stop fighting me."

She *did* try to fight him, but it was no good. Now that he held her, all the desire that she had known before with him suddenly was kindled.

"No, Ken—you and Marianne—"

"Goddamn it, stop it!" he erupted. "I'm here! *Here! Not* with Marianne. *Not* with anyone else, but here with *you*. Isn't that proof enough? I came here because I want *my* woman. Is that clear?"

His display of anger frightened her for a moment. She stood before him, knowing that paleness etched itself around her lips, and feeling her fear as she saw the anger in his eyes. He was a powerful, certain, demanding man. He knew possession. He had possessed her before, and he would again. She saw it in his expression and heard it in the masculine impatience and anger in his voice.

He smiled tightly and hooked fingers in the front of her low-cut gown. With force he ripped the dress down so that she stood erect and frightened in half-nudity, her breasts firm with the pink tips rising in uncontrolled and strange excitement. For fleeting seconds her fright and anger at the crude gesture he had made was eclipsed by an odd and powerful surge of pride in her body and in her femininity. She knew that she stood straighter and that she thrust out her breasts in feminine defiance, and that she was proud to feel the erectness of the nipples.

For the first time in their relationship a tinge of respect came into Nytrack's voice.

"Jesus! But you *are* a woman!" he said softly.

She experienced an awkward moment as they stood thus; she with the torn gown dropping about her waist, the strapless bra hanging disorderly, the slight coolness of the room an active thing against her bared breasts. She waited, not knowing exactly what to say or do.

The decision was taken from her.

"Now we'll go to bed," he said.

"Please, no," Kima whispered, some inner compulsion revolting against the desire that was sweeping over her. She retreated. "No, Ken."

He picked her up and buried his face against her breast. She shuddered and after seconds she clutched his head to her. He laughed softly and carried her into the bedroom and put her upon the bed.

He undressed her, not too gently, tearing silk lace to finally look at her nudity.

Kima shut her eyes and tried not to think. She was confused. Ken Nytrack was like no other man she had known: his objectives were in a world almost unknown to her; he talked in huge sums of money; he dealt with many employees; he had wealth, power, appetite and a confident ability to get what he wanted.

He wanted her. He would have her again, as he had taken her in Las Vegas. At the moment she was completely powerless to stop him.

He took her vigorously and hungrily. The very ardor of his masculine demands aroused her own desire to unusual heights.

She responded to him completely, almost angrily, matching his vigor with her own; mysteriously transforming the mating into an odd combat between male and female.

When they finished she was completely exhausted, and when he moved away from her she saw the long, angry scratches upon his back, where pencil-thin lines of blood were beginning to show.

Now, however, she knew a difference. After their love-making in Las Vegas there had been a satisfaction and happiness. Ken had been something completely different to her then, a man with whom she thought herself in love, a man who was offering love. This night she felt no happiness; only a sickening suspicion that she had been used.

After a time he left her, his endearments and departing kiss seeming forced and false. She didn't comment, nor move. She heard her door close and she stared at the ceiling, not bothering to cover herself. The room felt warm now.

"Why did you do that?" she asked herself. "Why?"

Now, in a moment of exhaustion and truth, she made herself admit that she suspected that Ken Nytrack did not love her, but found her desirable and enjoyable. In that event, she was doing little more than selling herself.

The thought was harsh and she quickly tried to evade it. She would *not* let herself believe it! She had been in love with Ken. She must have been, or it couldn't have turned out as it did. Only she was beginning to recall the stories and rumors and warnings about him.

After a long time she slept.

She had a late call the following day and when she arrived she was surprised to find Nytrack looking fresh and energetic—even after his early call, a half-day of hard work and very little sleep.

He greeted her almost casually. Marianne was talking solemnly with him. Kima caught the last part of the conversation.

"I simply don't want you to become ill, Ken," Marianne said. "You didn't act well last night when we had to leave early. I'm worried about you, and I want you to take care of yourself."

"I will," Nytrack said impatiently. "Kima, are you ready for the bedroom scene?"

"Yes," she nodded. *So he had feigned illness to break up his previous evening with Marianne to come to the hotel!* She knew that he was slightly embarrassed by her overhearing the last part of Marianne's admonishments.

He motioned to Rick Glasgow, who joined them with a welcoming smile for Kima. Nytrack said, "Rick, you and Kima are in a clinch when Marianne comes in and finds you. This is largely your scene, Kima. You're playing around with another woman's man—you're caught—you know you're guilty, try to conceal it—"

"Just be yourself," Marianne interrupted with a false laugh. "You hardly need a rehearsal for this situation."

Nytrack turned to the redheaded woman. "For Christ's sake, Marianne, knock it off! Please?"

The actress shrugged.

But Kima had experienced enough. She smiled at Nytrack and said, "You want me to really feel the part—to arouse enough emotions to carry it off—as you were telling me late last night?"

The reference to the preceding night had its calculated effect. She saw Rick Glasgow look at her curiously, but the sudden flare of anger on Marianne's face was the prize that Kima sought. She had scored.

She glanced at Nytrack. He was not smiling, and the familiar look of amusement in his eyes was not there. He glared coldly at Kima, and he carefully avoided Marianne's eyes.

He said, "Let's walk through this scene."

"Yes, let's," Marianne said icily. "I didn't get a rehearsal last night."

Almost stiffly they went through the action of the scene, voices tight, movements unnatural, the tenseness of the previous moment heavy upon all of them.

"We'll take a half-hour break," Nytrack decided. "Kima—wait. I want to talk with you."

Marianne gave him another angry look and left the set. Glasgow wandered toward his dressing room. Kima waited for Nytrack to speak.

"That wasn't very smart," he said.

"How much do you expect me to take from her, Ken?"

"Sure, I know. But it wasn't smart. We have to work with her. She'll take it out on you, and that means trouble with scenes and finishing the picture."

"Are you afraid of her?" Kima asked bluntly. "And incidentally, just where *does* she stand with you—and where do *I* stand?"

"If you don't know after last night—"

"That isn't an answer."

"Goddamn it, that's the answer you get! Is that clear? You're not to worry about Marianne. You're to worry about doing your part in this picture, being what I want you to be, and not deliberately antagonizing Marianne."

"God, you're colossal! You really are, Ken!" she snapped. "Just what do you think I am? Something left over from the slave girls when Caesar was in fashion in this city?"

Slowly he relaxed his angry expression and the smile of amusement returned. "You emote," he said, almost to himself. "With some seasoning, some experience in turning it on and off, Kima, you've got it. Truly you have."

"What has that to do with Marianne and you and me?" she demanded.

"A lot of work for you in this picture—while you're here. In the future, who knows?"

Before she could say more he left her alone on the empty set. She returned to a dressing room and angrily smoked a cigarette until she was called.

They worked hard on the scene for two hours. Ken Nytrack had been right. Marianne moved in with an experienced touch and virtually stole every scene from Kima during rehearsal.

"Kima, you have to be stronger," Nytrack told her curtly. "Let's try it again."

Finally he was satisfied, and by that time the three participants in the scene were barely speaking to one another. Marianne addressed all her remarks to Glasgow. Kima did the same. Glasgow wearily served as a balance wheel and finally it was through his effort and work that the scene managed to come off to Nytrack's satisfaction.

They were through for the day. Without another word to Kima, Nytrack left with Marianne, who was being highly aloof and angry.

"I'll drive you to the hotel when you're ready," Rick told Kima.

"Thanks, Rick. I'd like that."

In his sports car his voice emphasized the seriousness of his thoughts. "You made a dangerous enemy this afternoon, Kima. Marianne can hurt you."

"It wasn't just this afternoon," Kima said. "Or hadn't you noticed before? Her claws have been out a long time."

"I noticed," he said. "Was he there when I took you home?"

She glanced at him. It was none of his business, but he knew well enough that Ken Nytrack had been waiting for her.

"Yes," she admitted.

"I'd heard rumors about a thing between you two," Rick said. "Didn't know how far it actually went. Do you care to tell me?"

"I can't, Rick. I truly can't. I don't know."

"You're a level-headed girl. Don't get in a mess over this. There are other producers and other directors. You have talent. Do you understand that—that you have talent?"

She nodded. "I think I know," she said. "Yes."

"Then cherish it."

"Maybe the first thing I'd better do is finish my part in this picture," she said calmly. "After that—any suggestions?"

"Maybe," he said. "And about Ken—" He hesitated as he neatly passed several slower cars. "I guess you and I are good enough friends to say it. I mean—"

"Don't." She smiled crookedly. "It's been said before. 'Look out for Ken Nytrack.' In the down-to-earth language of some Californians I know, he is supposed to be a son-of-a-bitch."

Rick laughed. "Quote and unquote," he nodded. "There's a party tonight. Almost everyone will be there—including Ken, Marianne and a fairly representative crowd of other movie people, a few of the nobility, some unsavory characters, some very wealthy internationalites, and—of course—peeping over the walls, the *paparazzi*."

"You mean a real Roman orgy?" she grinned.

"Madam, it could be just that. Want to go?"

"I'd love to go. Looks as if I haven't a date with anyone else tonight. And I think I'd break it if I did!"

CHAPTER TEN

I T WAS A PARTY such as she never had attended before, in an estate that had a garden enclosed by a towering wall. The night was balmy. The activities were startling at times, and as the night grew older it seemed that more guests were continually arriving.

As Rick had said, the *paparazzi* were in evidence, on top of the garden wall, and occasionally among the guests in the garden or in the house itself. No one seemed to mind nor care too much. Those who did managed to protect themselves from the inquisitive camera lens.

Frequently Kima was separated from Rick, but that appeared to be expected at a party like this. For a few moments she had been with Ken, but he had told her he was tired and thought he'd leave early. There was no mention of seeing her later.

She saw Marianne several times, once in serious conversation with a handsome young Italian. Marianne appeared to be giving instructions, and the young man nodded emphatically and smilingly.

Consequently when the young man approached Kima later, bringing a drink to her, she was a little curious.

"Miss Shannon?" he asked in studied English. "Miss Kima Shannon, the Hollywood starlet?"

"That's debatable," she smiled, inspecting the smooth face, the dark eyes, the poise and good looks that reminded her of the old Valentino reruns she had seen on TV.

He frowned as if he had detected displeasure in her voice. "Hollywood starlet is—perhaps not the right phrase?"

"Hollywood starlet is usually a myth," she told him. She took the drink he offered her and sampled it. It was very strong and had a slightly odd taste.

"What is it?" she asked.

"Who knows?" he smiled charmingly. "The man who mixed it says it is his own—some brandy, some wine, some bitters. I like it."

"Who are you?"

"My name is Vittorio Truzzo. The Americans call me Vic."

"You're an actor?"

"Only in a minor way. I have had one small part in a picture that you have not seen. Very few have. But I have several lines in a new one, and I am certain that I shall eventually have good parts."

She smiled. "With your looks, you should, Vic. I suppose a great many people have told you that you look like Valentino."

He smiled deprecatingly. "I am taller than he was, and that is good. As for the rest ..." He shrugged elaborately. "Who knows?"

The drinks had been very powerful, or possibly it was the accumulation of all that she had allowed herself during the evening. She felt a little dizzy and drowsy. She shuddered. "That drink made me dizzy," she complained.

He took her drink and gave her his own.

"Here. Sometimes another strong drink helps."

"I don't—"

"Drink it," he smiled. "It'll help. I assure you."

She laughed and drank it. Maybe he was right. A strong drink might overcome strong drink! She felt like shaking her head to clear it, but she was definitely very dizzy and drowsy now.

"How come …?" She began to ask a question and found it difficult to talk. "You … you and Marianne?"

"A charming woman," he smiled. "Most charming."

"You look—looked—so serious!" She wished she had not taken the second drink. The people about them, the garden, the lights were whirling and her eyes were refusing to focus well.

"You're not feeling well?" he asked.

"Dizzy."

He put a strong hand under her arm and led her away from the crowd. "We'll walk in the quiet. There is another garden and we'll go there and be alone. You can sit down and the fresh air and quiet will help."

"This—I mean, this doesn't sound—" She wasn't certain what she wanted to say. It was easier to say nothing and let him lead her. She was aware that they were alone and that she could still hear the sounds of the party. But the party was behind them, on the other side of the wall and now they were in another garden alone. He was leading her along a path between bushes.

They came to a small clearing where a fountain was white in moonlight. There was a marble bench. She wanted to sit there. She was dizzy and confused. The taste of the drinks remained in her mouth. There was something wrong about the taste.

They had stopped walking and stood beside the marble bench. The man with the dark eyes faced her, looking down at her, his hands lightly on her shoulders.

"You are lovely," he said softly. "You are a lovely woman … a lovely woman."

An insidious lassitude crept through her so that she was singularly defenseless. Her arms hung listlessly, her gaze was almost dully fixed upon Truzzo's face. His voice lulled and soothed her. She bowed her head and leaned against him so that her forehead was against his chest. She shut her eyes and felt as if she were floating.

An arm came around her, strong and supporting, bending her in at the waist to him. A hand came beneath her chin and tilted it up so that she looked into his face again when she opened her eyes.

His face came very close and out of focus. She shut her eyes again as she felt his full, warm, insinuating mouth cover her lips. Slowly her lassitude became submission and she opened to his kiss and let her body come loose and close against him.

Truzzo held her away again with hands on her shoulders. She was only dimly aware of the scene, the white marble, the solitude, the heavy foliage of bushes about them in the garden nook, and the moonlight.

"Stand still," he whispered. "You are like a statue. You could be a statue in the garden. Like this ..."

The urge to stop him was there, but the drinks and the lassitude robbed her of strength to resist. She stood motionless as he opened her dress and slipped the bodice down over her shoulders to her waist; as he freed her brassiere and pulled it down. She remained motionless, nude to the waist, even as a statue of moon-bathed marble might have been in the garden.

"Beautiful!" Truzzo breathed. With an effort she focused her eyes upon his face and saw the intensity of his dark eyes as he looked at her. "A woman's breasts," he whispered. "Young and beautiful ... made for caressing hands and lips."

He held her back over an arm so that he could bend to her. She shuddered as she felt his kiss upon her throat, and as his lips explored her breasts.

A cupped hand and lips became active so that she shuddered again and gasped. Her head fell back loosely and her arms became limp, almost as if she were in a faint—except for the instinctive arching of her body toward him in their standing embrace.

"Ah! *Cara mia!*" Truzzo whispered. "I wish—"

Suddenly from the darkness near them came the sound of voices, most of them male, but one of them female. Something flashed in Kima's eyes. Truzzo swore softly in Italian and one of his hands squeezed angrily about a breast. She moaned from the unexpected pain.

The flashes came with increased rapidity. Truzzo kissed her hard, grinding his mouth against hers, his hands taking new liberties with her body.

She tried to break free, but she was alarmingly weak and confused. She drew back from him with desperate strength and saw a young woman beside them, dark eyes flashing in the moonlight.

"No! No!" the woman said angrily. She forced herself between Truzzo and Kima. Truzzo stepped back and smiled. Lights flashed. The woman spat something in angry Italian at Truzzo and he laughed. His laugh brought a response of guffaws and masculine giggles from around them. The woman snarled more angry words at him.

Truzzo spoke rapidly, almost placatingly, in Italian and laughed again, as if he were sharing a joke with the young, dark woman. The woman relaxed a little and nodded. She stepped away from Kima and a humorless smile revealed white, even teeth.

"*Sì!*" the young woman said and nodded. "*Sì!*" Abruptly she, too, laughed and one of her hands slashed out in a vicious slap across Kima's face. The lights flashed again.

Kima recoiled but the other woman sprang after her, uttering harsh, vindictive-sounding Italian words. Kima fell and the young woman sprang upon her, straddling Kima, her own bare thighs white in the rapidly flashing lights about them.

The masculine voices rose in soft shouts of encouragement, perverted giggles and delighted cries. The lights flashed continuously. Kima tried to protect her face from the other woman's hands.

Then a laughing Truzzo was lifting the other woman away. The lights flashed. Kima tried desperately not to sink into a great darkness. She was on the edge of it. She was going to be ill. She was nauseated. The bitterness! She remembered the odd and bitter taste of the drinks Truzzo had given her.

Like a spotlight coming through a fog, and out of her receding consciousness, came a single, phantom word: *"Drugged"* ... *"drugged"* ...

Somewhere from a distance someone called her name. The voice sounded far away. The laughter and giggling about her became silenced. A hand reached down and obscenely manhandled her breasts and lights flashed very near to her, almost into her face.

The sound of her name being called was nearer now. The voices around her became subdued in hurried warnings. There were a few more flashes, hands manhandled her again, briefly and roughly, and then the voice that called her name was quite close. She heard feet scurry away in retreat as her assailants fled. She tried to get up, but she was too ill and weak.

"Kima! Kima! For God's sake!"

Kima looked up into the face of Rick Glasgow. He bent over her and helped her up. She turned her back to him and awkwardly pulled up her brassiere and the bodice of her dress.

He hovered behind her, asking questions in a perturbed and angry voice. Finally she could face him and she sat on the marble bench as another wave of dizziness and nausea came over her.

Rick Glasgow said, "I missed you and started to look. I couldn't find you at the party and then I saw flashes over here. *Paparazzi.* I got worried and came over. Usually where they are something is happening."

"Something was happening all right," Kima said bitterly. She breathed deeply and it cleared her head a little. "Rick, do you suppose we could find some black coffee at the party?"

"Certainly. Possibly some *espresso* in the kitchen."

"Let's. Then I'll tell you about it."

Walking unsteadily, Kima was glad to have Rick's supporting arm as they left the deserted garden and returned to the party. They skirted couples and groups and found a deserted arbor not far from the lighted mansion.

"Wait here," he told her. "I'll find the coffee."

He was gone about ten minutes and returned with a large cup of the steaming, strong liquid.

"I found the kitchen," he explained. "Here—it will help." She sipped it tentatively and found that it seemed to clear her mind and restore some of her strength. Finally she put down the cup and accepted a cigarette from Glasgow.

"Now, Kima—I want to know what happened," he said.

"I don't exactly know. But I'll tell you as much as I can."

He listened attentively until she was finished. "This Italian—this Vic Truzzo—was talking with Marianne?"

"Yes. Does it mean anything?"

"It damned well might," Rick Glasgow growled. "I know him. The girl who attacked you probably is his wife. They're an unscrupulous pair—ambitious, trying to make the news, hungry for money and careers. They'll do anything. And the bitterness in the drink, the way you felt and all the rest of it—it sounds like a drug."

"But it doesn't make sense!"

"I'm afraid it does," Rick said thoughtfully. "I mean it looks as if Marianne has been up to something."

"Why don't I find her and ask her?" Kima said angrily. "I'm becoming sick and tired of that woman."

"No use. She and Ken left a half-hour ago."

"Then will you take me home, Rick? I've sort of had it."

"Party's becoming a bore, anyhow. The strip-tease bit will start soon—if our primitive dancing blonde hasn't already begun. Would you like to stay a little longer to watch the so-called orgy?"

"It looks more like an ordinary drunken brawl to me," Kima said, managing a smile. "But if they want to call it an orgy—well, when in Rome, do as the Romans do."

"You always manage a smile. That helps me to be very fond of you."

Instinotively she stood on her toes to kiss him. "Thank you, Rick," she said. "I'm sorry I'm not the kind of girl who would invite you home to bed now. I mean, I almost wish I were, because you're so nice."

"A nicely turned compliment—and parried pass," he grinned. "Come on. Let's go home. We may need sleep before tomorrow comes."

"That sounds almost ominous."

"It is, Kima. I don't like what happened."

It turned out to be much, much more ominous than either of them was to anticipate. By four o'clock the following afternoon Nytrack had left the studio and called a conference in his hotel suite. Rick brought Kima.

She was surprised to find Cliff Cation, the cynical, hardbitten public relations man with Nytrack. Immediately after their arrival in Rome he had said good-bye to Kima and had embarked on a swing through West European countries to begin setting up publicity for the picture. He appeared to be very tired now. He was unshaven and obviously disgusted.

Nytrack looked at Kima with eyes holding only his anger. "Do you know why you're here?" he asked.

Kima took a deep breath to steady herself. She looked directly into Nytrack's eyes and said, "No, I don't know why I'm here. I think you'd better explain."

"Knock it off, baby," Nytrack snapped. "You know damned well what it's all about. Take a look." He picked up some glossy press photographs from a coffee table and tossed them into her lap.

Kima began to run through the pictures and felt her cheeks burn with a blush. The first glossies showed her in Vic Truzzo's arms, nude to the waist, her head back as the dark, young Italian caressed her. The pictures were almost a sequence that gave the impression that the couple had been surprised in the most intimate preliminaries to love-making.

Then came pictures of the young Italian woman, anger showing plainly on her face as she forced her way between the couple. A long series of pictures showed the flurry of fighting that culminated with the Italian woman straddling Kima as she slapped the American actress' face.

With fingers that moved almost like parts of a complex piece of automation machinery, Kima went through the small stack of pictures, feeling disgust and sickness rising in her.

The final shots were close-ups of male hands obscenely handling Kima's breasts, and the grimace of pain on her face, which might be misinterpreted by some gloating eyes as a grimace of ecstasy.

Even as she experienced the shock of seeing herself in the lurid pictures, she realized that quite a few of them had been skillfully taken so that the full extent of her nudity was only suggested and not outright censorable—especially the pictures showing the young Italian woman's attack upon Kima.

Rick looked over her shoulder. "Damn them!" he growled. "They can sell these."

Kima threw the pictures to the floor as if they were suddenly red-hot. "They don't mean anything!" she cried. "That man—his name is Vittorio Truzzo—gave me some drinks. They must have been drugged. I don't know what was happening afterward."

"I'll tell you what was happening!" Nytrack exclaimed. "You were about to lay that Italian punk in the garden and you got caught! I'll tell you what happened, baby—you posed for as sweet a set of semi-pornographic shots as any starlet has come up with for a long time around here—or anywhere!"

"That's not true, damn you, that's not true! You listen to me and—"

"Do you know where prints of some of those pictures are right now?" Nytrack asked. "The ones that are only suggestive—not completely censorable?"

She stared at him, silenced by the coldness in his voice.

"I'll tell you," he said. "They're on jets en route to every damned scandal sheet in the United States—to all the magazines that feature the words 'confidential' and 'exposé' and 'peep' and all the scandal phrases. The more toned down versions are going to newspapers and news services and news magazines where they can be a little more sedate, but just as damning. And to the fan magazines, the picture magazines, the trades—everywhere and anywhere that a *paparazzi* can sell a picture and a story."

"But there isn't a story!" Kima protested.

"They have a story to go with the pictures, baby. I called Cation back to try to stop some of it, but he can't. I had an investment. But it's over the dam. The story makes the pictures—makes them *really* news."

"What story?" Kima angrily cried at him. "*What* story?"

"A honey, baby. A real honey. The young, happy Italian couple, not married very long. She may even be pregnant—they're not certain yet, but think she is. And he is just breaking into pictures and showing great promise. She already is cast for a role in a picture that may get some real attention. All nice—until you come along and try to steal him. At a party. In a next-door garden. The wife followed you—the *paparazzi* smelled a story and followed her. And she caught up with both of you. But she didn't take it out on him! She's forgiving *him*. *You're* to blame, baby! He's pretending to protect you, but everyone knows he's just being gentlemanly. What else is a guy going to do when a starlet tries to seduce him in a garden? Hell, baby—you've had it. You've really had it."

"What do you mean?" she whispered.

"I mean," said Nytrack, "that as soon as the story and these pictures hit the public you become a lousy little tramp who tried to break up a fine Italian marriage. The story will tell it. The pictures will prove it."

He hesitated and shook his head in profound disgust.

"And the pictures that the magazines and newspapers *can't* use," he said, "they'll be passed around, too. The smut dealers. Those pictures are sweethearts for that trade. The boys will love them—your Hollywood starlet face is nice and clear so they can recognize you but that guy Truzzo kept his back to the camera in the rough ones. Oh, you'll give the boys their kicks, baby! *Here I am, boys—look me over and see how I play!*"

Kima stared at him. "What do you want me to do?" she asked, trying to maintain a calm in the face of panic.

"Do? How in hell should *I* know? You took that guy into the garden to lay him! You got caught. And now you pay. *Do?* You go home, baby! We'll pay the fare. But you're out. I do mean *out*—of the picture, the industry and TV. I can't use pornographic stars or publicized tramps in my pictures—nor can any other legitimate producer."

She listened to him, wondering if he actually believed what he was saying, or if he spoke from hurt pride. For the moment she was almost too numb to actually understand what he did say.

"Why did they do it to me?" she asked.

"Why did *you* do it to *them?*" Nytrack retorted.

"I saw that man talking with Marianne—"

Nytrack lit a cigarette in an angry gesture. "Leave her out of it."

"Then I'm fired?"

"Yes, baby, you're fired."

"I'll call Milo. I don't know about our contract."

"There's a morality clause."

"I still don't know why they did it."

Rick answered her. "They're the injured ones—you tried to break up the family, they say. Of course they did it for publicity. They'll never get as much so easily."

"And I wonder how much Marianne paid them?" Kima said.

Nytrack stood. "Get out of here, baby. Keep going. You're nothing but a chippy."

She smiled tightly at him, knowing that she was white with anger.

"Everyone is right about you," she said softly. "You—Mr. Nytrack—are a first-class son-of-a-bitch!"

She turned and walked out of the room to a small alcove at the end of a hallway. A few moments later Rick found her and handed her a handkerchief so that she could dry her eyes.

"Kima, I'm terribly sorry. Let this blow over. Keep in touch. I think something can be worked out later. He's only right about one thing."

"One thing?" she asked dubiously.

"That you have talent. He's right about that. If you asked him now, he'd still admit that. He'd *have* to admit it."

CHAPTER ELEVEN

M ILO GINZ SAT behind his desk in Hollywood and looked at Kima with sympathy and consideration in his eyes.

"It's no use, Kima, darling," he said. "PAK invoked the morality clause, too. I can't get you anything—maybe a voice-over TV spot. Maybe not. You're like poison—this I got to tell you."

"But, Milo, I didn't *do* those things! It's all a lie! I—"

He hushed her with a raised hand, and again his sympathy was sincerely reflected in his expression.

"This I know, child—this I know. To me you are not poison, nor to Sam, nor to my brother-in-law Sahnstein who would like to use you but can't. You are poison to the public—the public that doesn't like homebreakers, which it thinks you are—which I know you aren't."

He shook his head and pointed to magazines and newspapers he had spread on his desk.

"Headlines like these, yet: 'ITALIAN WIFE ACCUSES STARLET' ... 'WHAT HAPPENED BEHIND GARDEN WALLS' ... 'STARLET SHANNON GETS WORKED OVER BY WIFE' ... 'KIMA CALLED SPOUSE-STEALER' ... 'WIFE TAKES MATTERS IN OWN HANDS—LITERALLY' ... 'ITALIAN ACTRESS SAYS KIMA SEDUCED HUSBAND' ... 'STARLET CAUGHT AT ORGY.' "

Ginz snorted in obvious disgust. "Even the decent press carried pictures and stories. The trades announced Nytrack fired you. The leagues of decency—or whatever they call them yet—are slapping at you. And the pictures those *paparazzi* got—ach!"

"Milo, what am I going to do? When I got the contract I bought things. I moved. I've spent money. Income tax is so high—everything. I only have a few hundred dollars left. I have to find a job."

The agent avoided her eyes. "I don't know, Kima. Maybe a job in something else ..."

"I could go back to New York."

"The stories and pictures are everywhere. New York ... here ... Rome. Running away won't help. The industry doesn't want you right now."

"And you simply can't place me, Milo?"

"My right arm I would give, but I can't. A loan—I can give you a loan, you should need it. A role I can't. Maybe a cheap night club, but talent like that I don't handle. You're too good. Talent you got, Kima. I'm sick with it. I tell my wife, Sarah, I am sick for Kima Shannon—that I can't do more for her right now."

"I guess there are other jobs—stores, offices ..."

"Maybe for a while that is best. Maybe a year. Then this may blow over. Maybe something can be worked out. The morality clause rap is hard to beat, darling."

"Yes, Milo. Thanks. I won't take more of your time. I know you've done your best for me—and you're busy."

"Keep in touch. You're still my client, Kima. Keep in touch. You hear? And maybe you try to find another job? You type, maybe? Shorthand?"

"You ought to see me as a carhop." She smiled thinly. "I'll keep in touch. And if anything should come up—"

"I'll call you, darling. You check with me every week or so until things work out."

Sam Berill, looking thinner and more tired than ever, helped her find a cheap one-room-and-kitchenette apartment and moved her in his dilapidated car. His anger about her predicament had driven him to the bottle and he voiced his feelings in a bitterly acid voice.

"Damned scum," he growled. "Blackmailers, scandalmongers..."

Kima sat on the daveno in the room she had just rented and surveyed her belongings that he had brought up. She didn't know where she could put all the luggage and wardrobe she had bought on the strength of her contract with Nytrack.

Evidently Sam had been thinking about her financial affairs, too. "How did you come out on your contract?" he asked, lighting a fresh cigarette and sprawling his long length into a chair.

"Not good," she told him. "Nytrack had a stiff morality clause. I get paid for the actual time I was on the job. No more. He can cancel all the rest and he has."

"Feeling real low, Kima?"

"Very. I spent a lot. I have a few hundred left."

"I've got a few bucks. Let me know—"

"I'll find something. I have to. Maybe in an office somewhere."

"Know any businessmen?"

She shook her head, and then remembered Bill Rold. He dealt in taxes, and he probably had an office and staff. He might even have a job for her. She was about to tell her idea to Sam when she remembered that Sam had not been enthusiastic about Rold. Besides, Sam already had drunk too much, and he could become a problem if she didn't get him to eat.

"Let's have some dinner," she suggested.

"Fine. I know a little bar where we can—"

"No bar, Sam. Just food. And plenty of it. Good and cheap. if we can find such a place."

"Hamburgers?"

"The great American dish," she sighed. "I'd rather have an old-fashioned New England boiled dinner—it would somehow be solid and comforting. But I'll settle for a hamburger. Is there a place near here?"

"A few blocks away."

They ate hamburgers in his car and then he took her home. She stopped him from getting out of his car.

"Would you mind too much, Sam? I'm tired and want to sort things out and get to bed early. You've helped a lot—and I know you're tired, too."

"A girl's got a right to privacy," he grinned. "I'll call you tomorrow."

He leaned forward suddenly and kissed her on the tip of her nose. She cupped his thin, man's face in her hands and kissed him gently and firmly on the mouth.

"That's for helping, and being what you are, Sam," she said.

When she looked back from the entrance to the apartment building, he still was in the car, watching her. She waved and he lifted a hand. She went inside, trying to hold back tears again, and wondering why she suddenly felt so dreadfully lonesome.

Bill Rold's office surprised her a trifle. Somehow she had expected that it might resemble the suite of a young executive as conceived for a movie set. Actually, it was pleasantly functional. In a large room clerks and machine operators worked industriously. A very plain and pleasant middle-aged woman greeted her. She called Rold on an intercom and said that he would see Kima.

They went down a short hallway and the receptionist opened the door to Rold's office. Kima went in.

Rold got up from behind a desk laden with work and came forward. He took her hands and pressed them.

"Kima! I'm glad to see you." He led her to a chair beside his desk and then sat in his own chair behind the broad surface.

"I'm impressed," Kima smiled.

"So?" Rold asked with raised eyebrows.

Kima made a gesture to include the office and furnishings. "It all looks so functional."

He smiled with her. "It is. We do a big volume of business. We not only handle tax matters for a lot of the Hollywood crowd, but we have a good clientele among other professional people—doctors, decorators, dealers and others."

"I won't take much of your time. You're busy."

"What can I do for you, Kima?"

"I want a job."

He looked at her thoughtfully. "I've seen the pictures and the stories," he said. "I've heard what Ken did. I understand that you've made the famous black list."

"That's right, Bill. The stories—the pictures—they're all misleading. It wasn't that way. But the very fact that they're using the pictures and story makes it true for the public and the industry. I'm looking for some other kind of job."

He nodded in understanding. "I guess the question changes a little then. Not the old cliché, 'What have you done?' but 'What can you do?' "

"Not much, I'm afraid. I mean, no skills of importance. I can type. I could answer a telephone and be a receptionist. I could clerk, possibly be a waitress. I don't know, Bill. I just thought that you might have a place—or know someone …"

"We have no openings here," he said thoughtfully. "But I'll check some of our clients."

"Will you, Bill?"

"Certainly!" He glanced at his wristwatch. "Look, darling—I don't want to rush you, but I've an appointment and a luncheon date. All business. But I'm free tonight—if you are. How about dinner? I'll make some calls this afternoon and report."

"What unemployed gal can afford to turn down a free dinner?" Kima smiled.

"Good." He grinned, and got up. "Tonight then. Where do you live?"

She told him. "I just moved there—economy gesture."

"As a tax expert I commend you!" Rold put an arm around her as he took her to the office door. "And look, darling—don't worry?"

He sounded reassuring and she left the office feeling much better. Even the rejections she had during the rest of the day in her search for a job didn't seem quite so bad when she remembered Bill Rold. He was a man with many contacts. He probably would find something for her.

They ate at a place on the coast highway.

Midway through dinner Rold told her that he had made several calls about jobs, but that it would be a few days before he would know if any of the calls bore fruit.

"It takes time," he told her. "But tell me about Rome. What happened? I'd like the true story."

She told him and he listened attentively, asking a question now and then.

"The pictures are pretty bad," he said. "They did a good job of smearing you, Kima."

Suddenly something in his eyes and voice disturbed her. She looked across the table without smiling.

"Bill," she asked, "you do believe me, don't you?"

Was there a slight hesitation? Did his eyes narrow just a trifle? She remembered the episode involving the TV star in Vegas. Did he think that he might have been wrong about her?

"Bill," she said evenly, "I am not a tramp. Let's get that straight? For sure? I am *not* a tramp."

His quick smile looked sincere enough. "You don't have to tell me, Kima. I was there once. Fisticuffs and all. Remember?"

"I thought you might have changed your mind. Those pictures *do* look bad, and the story *does* hang together."

He changed the subject and told her about some of his work. After dinner they drove along the coast for a while and then circled and came back over Mulholland Highway. It still was early when he parked near the apartment building.

"It's only a room and a kitchenette," she told him. "But I do have some bourbon, some vodka, gin and a little bit of Scotch. And it *is* early. Will you come up?"

"All right. Unless you'd rather go somewhere else for a while."

"No. I'm tired—and lonesome. I'd like to talk a while longer and have a drink or two."

Later he took a good look around the small apartment. "It isn't as bad as you make it out to be," he told her.

She was mixing drinks in the kitchenette. "That modern-looking couch makes into a fairly good bed—it's a daveno," she told him. "The TV works. It will do until my money runs out."

"Sure." He came over behind her and watched her make the drinks. She was very conscious of his closeness and she busied herself with the liquor, ice, and glasses, almost expectantly, as if she were waiting for him to do something.

When he moved, it was to put his arms around her from the back, cupping her breasts in his hands, and gently kissing her on the back of her neck. The sudden boldness of his movements almost shocked her. She stiffened and her hands became motionless in their task.

"Don't, Bill," she said. "You're spoiling things."

"This isn't because I believe those stories and pictures," he said. "It's because I've wanted to hold you and kiss you ever since that night in Vegas."

She placed her hands over his at her breasts and took them away as she moved out of his arms. She picked up a drink and turned to hand it to him.

"Did you have to tell me *that* way?" she asked.

"Isn't that one of the most natural ways for a man to tell a woman that he truly wants her?"

"Wanting a woman and caring about a woman are two different things, Bill."

"I wouldn't want you if I didn't care about you."

"You're turning words around. Let's take our drinks and sit down. Please?"

He smiled and they went to the daveno. She had turned on only a single shaded lamp and in the dim light the room looked better than it did in the glare of daylight.

Bill sipped at the drink, and put the glass on the coffee table in front of the daveno.

"What is it with you, Kima?" he asked. "I mean—really."

"I don't know what you mean, Bill."

"You know. You were in Vegas with Ken. That means one thing to me, and I can take it or leave it. Maybe you two had a thing going. But this stuff from Rome. How did you get in such a hell of a mess?"

"You mean, how did it happen unless I asked for it? Like with that TV hero at the party in Vegas? You think I—that I …?"

He shook his head. "No, I don't. I don't want to think that. I know people. I seldom make a mistake. Forget what I said."

Their silence almost became an embarrassment as they looked at one another.

"Bill, I'm not—" she faltered.

"I know it. Come here, baby." He gently pulled her to him and kissed her. For a few seconds she resisted him, but there seemed so little to resist. He was holding her and kissing her so gently and protectively.

"Why don't you stop worrying so much?" he asked softly.

"I'm scared; Bill. Old-fashioned scared. No job—and all this mess. I don't have anyone to really turn to and—"

"You might try me, Kima." He kissed her again and this time she felt tears come to her eyes. She *was* frightened and discouraged and uncertain. She *needed* to he held and kissed and comforted.

He turned her so that she swung her feet and legs up on the daveno and rested across his lap, her head cradled in the crook of his arm. He looked down at her and smiled. With his free hand he traced the tears down her cheeks and wiped them away.

"Let *me* do some of the worrying. Okay? And why don't you just relax and be held for a while? I've heard that it does a girl good to be held!"

"That's what they say, Bill."

"I'm sorry about the things I said. And I mean it—about caring for you."

He kissed her again and after a while the kiss became more than a friendly and affectionate gesture. Kima felt the strength of his arms about her and welcomed it. She wanted someone to sustain her right now. She was grateful. She put her arms around his neck and returned his kiss.

"Baby ..." he whispered. "I've wanted to kiss you since that night. Again ... again ..." His lips closed over her mouth in hard, searching kisses. Kima felt excitement stir within her as the restlessness of desire awakened. When his demanding mouth opened her lips to him, she involuntarily moved against him.

His free hand found the buttons of her blouse and his fingers quickly unbuttoned and pulled it aside. He found the straps of her slip and bra and slipped them down over her bare shoulders so that her breasts were free, as they had been in the pictures taken in Italy.

She tried to summon the effort to push herself up and to pull up the straps and bra and close the blouse, but somehow one arm was locked behind him, and now the hand of his arm around her neck caught her free wrist and held it. She was powerless to move.

"Don't ... please, Bill ... don't ..." This was almost as silly and amateurish as the fumbling skirmishes she had experienced in parked cars during high school days. Then the boys awkwardly had tried wrestling holds and tactics as they endeavored to take their adolescent liberties, and always she had managed to break free, or cool young and undisciplined ardor with a laugh or a cutting remark.

But it wasn't silly any more. Those nights long ago had been when she was a virgin; calm and certain in her determined morality. After she met Jimmy the world had changed for her. Then Clint Clinton had taught her that she was truly a woman in a sexual sense. Ken Nytrack had shown her how fully she could be awakened and how high the flame could soar for her. Now she realized that the defenses she once could rely upon were lacking. She felt powerless and defenseless.

His lips had strayed down from her mouth, over her throat to the full and rounded softness that awaited them. Despite her desperate wish to deny herself—and him—she found herself lifting against him. Her arms no longer fought against his strength, but were lax and compliant as her eyes shut and she threw back her head against his arm and welcomed his caresses.

Somehow they were on the floor and she pushed away from him.

"No, not here," she whispered. "The couch opens ..."

Silently they got up from the floor. She showed him how the daveno opened. He opened it and then turned and pulled her into a standing embrace, his hands upon her, seeking the secret of her clothing.

She helped him. Finally they were on the bed and he had turned out the light.

"This is crazy," Bill said huskily. "I didn't plan it this way. You've got to believe that, Kima."

"I know," she murmured, pressing her mouth against his throat. She did know that it was crazy. She had been attracted to this man from the moment she had met him, but this night he had awakened desires that she could not halt.

"I can't stop this now," he said. "You know that ..."

"Yes ... yes." She moved for him and there was a brief moment of exploration and adjustment. Their desire was mutual and intense so that there was no waiting, nor nuances of love-making. They made love desperately and with such abandon that they were spent and exhausted within moments.

"Bill ..." she whispered after it was finished. "Was it for real?"

"You know how it was," he told her. He moved from the bed and got cigarettes for them and returned to the bed. "I didn't intend that to happen, Kima."

Abruptly Kima was strangely displeased with herself and with him. "And now you're sorry?" she asked.

"No ... it isn't that. It's—well, let's skip it, baby."

She didn't speak for moments, smoking in silence. He remained away from her on the bed, not touching her, obviously satiated for the moment.

"It's getting late, Bill," she said. "You'd better go."

"I suppose so. Rough day tomorrow."

He left the bed and went into the bathroom for a few moments. He came out and dressed, returning to the bathroom mirror to knot his necktie. Kima got up and put on her skirt and blouse. Her nudity suddenly had embarrassed her. Bill came back into the room and took her briefly into his arms to kiss her.

"Call me, baby," he told her. "I'll keep after a job for you."

"When will I see you?"

"I'll let you know. I'm crowded for a few days. But call."

She went to the door with him and after he left she went into the bathroom. She saw the five twenty-dollar bills on the built-in dressing table.

She stared at the money. Certainly he had left it as a loan for her, to carry her over a rough spot. It couldn't be anything else. She saw a note beneath the money and read it: *Call it a loan, if you like. But it will help until you get a job.*

Looking up from the money she gazed at her reflection in the mirror.

"A loan?" she said softly. "Or payment for what he got! That's the way they pay whores."

Even as she recoiled from her thoughts the telephone rang. She went out to answer it.

Bill Rold said, "Baby, there's a hundred in the bathroom for you. I just got to thinking—I mean, don't take it wrong. I just want to help."

"I found the money, Bill. Thanks. I understand."

"Sure, now?"

"Yes, Bill. It's a loan. Nothing more. I'll call you tomorrow."

"I'd call *you*, but you'll probably be out. I mean, would you rather I called *you*?"

He sounded a little embarrassed, and she wondered where honesty began and ended. Why *had* he left the money?

"I'll call you," she said. "Good night, Bill."

After a moment she returned to the bathroom and drew a full tub of water. Somehow she wanted to be very clean. She felt the need for it.

It was almost midnight when she went to bed.

She had trouble going to sleep in the strange room. She stared at the ceiling and the light patterns that came through the window from street lights and a nearby flashing sign.

So much had happened in such a short time. It was only about a month ago that she had met Ken Nytrack. She had spent the night at Clint's beach house, and the next evening she was with Ken in Las Vegas. Then had come two weeks—a little more, perhaps—of hard, hard work getting ready for her big chance in *Ground Rules*. After that the trip to Rome—the days there—and back to Hollywood.

Now she had been home three days and the dream was ended. No job. No career. Nothing but her face, and what the editors would allow to be printed of her naked bosom, on the pages of scandal magazines.

Restlessly she turned in the bed until tears came from weariness, defeat and a strange fright. She buried her face in her pillow and sobbed.

She was almost asleep when an unexpected thought brought her wide-awake. Abruptly she sat up and turned on a bed lamp. With a frightened concentration she counted back over the days. The fast, fast days that had been so crowded, so hectic, until they became weeks.

She shut her eyes and fiercely tried to remember. She never had kept track. Not since Jimmy. There had been no reason. Now she desperately tried to recall a date, an incident—and at last she did.

She had stopped at a drugstore near her apartment for the feminine purchase she suddenly needed to make. She had no change and they had cashed a small check for her. The check stubs would tell!

Instantly she was out of bed and at her handbag. Rapidly she checked through the check records until she found the one listed "Drug store—cash" with the date and amount.

There was a small calendar in the checkbook. Carefully she counted back to the date of the purchase in the drugstore. She counted twice and then slowly closed the book and replaced it in her handbag.

For the first time she realized that she had not menstruated for six weeks!

Frantically she thought back. With Ken there had been precautions—even in Rome. When a woman senses that she may be vulnerable to a man's desires, she may take precautions even while she fights the possibility of yielding. She had with Ken.

"Clint," she thought. She had been with Clint a month ago— two weeks after her last cycle had started. In midcycle she could be impregnated. She hadn't really realized how dangerous it was that night. She did remember asking him to take precautions, and he hadn't.

"Clint got me pregnant that night!" she whispered in the darkness.

She looked about her wildly in the strange room, more frightened than she ever had been. She had to calm herself, to think. She went to the kitchenette. Sam had left a bottle half-filled with bourbon.

Her hand trembled as she poured a stiff drink into a water tumbler.

The liquor was raw-tasting, but it felt warm and soothing She drank the full drink and then another. She went to bed and shut her eyes. The bourbon spread its warmth through her body and she no longer was frightened. The room began to whirl, but she didn't bother to open her eyes. It was easier to let the room whirl.

"I'll see a doctor tomorrow," she said to the dark room. "But I am—I'm pregnant ..."

She started to sob again and finally slept.

CHAPTER TWELVE

FROM THE TELEPHONE BOOK's classified section she selected an obstetrician whose office was fairly close to her apartment. She called and got an appointment for that morning.

Before she went to the doctor's office she visited a variety store and selected a cheap wedding band at the jewelry counter. She slipped the ring on the proper finger, remembering how she had done this once before when she was in New York and sought contraceptive information. Ironically she thought that she would not be about to make the visit she planned if she had used what she had learned during that other visit.

Somehow she had expected the doctor to be elderly and she was surprised to be confronted by a relatively young man. He smiled and glanced at the card his receptionist had filled out for Kima.

"Mrs. Shannon?" he said. She had decided to use the surname. It was as good as any. "K. Shannon. Is that K-a-y or K for Katherine?"

She looked at him sharply, suddenly realizing that he may have seen the adverse pictures and the stories. Was he probing? Evidently he connected her with no scandal stories. He seemed to be merely asking for information.

"K-a-y," she said. Then she added, "My husband's name is George. He's a salesman."

"And now …?" he smiled, questioning her reason for being there.

"I may be pregnant."

"Very well … we'll make an examination and tests."

An hour later she left his office. The doctor would not be positive until he received laboratory reports in a few days, but he was strongly suspicious that she was pregnant. She was to call.

She returned to the apartment and called Bill Rold. He was away from his office. She tried to get Sam, without luck. Once again she felt frightened. She wanted to talk with someone; just to be with someone and not alone.

In the kitchenette she found several drinks left in the bottle of bourbon and she poured a stiff one. It helped. She poured another and finally a third. She began to feel them and some of her fright and worry disappeared. She needed to have company, though.

There was a small cocktail bar down the street. She had stopped there for cigarettes and it looked like a neighborhood place. She had seen girls there alone; girls who looked as if they might work in offices, or stores, or as extras.

Before she left the apartment she took off the variety store wedding band, and hid all but ten dollars of her money with her checkbook in a dresser drawer. She couldn't afford to spend too much, and if she was drinking, that could happen all too easily.

In the cocktail bar she found three or four couples, some single girls and several lone men. High fidelity FM music had been substituted for the customary juke box, and the atmosphere was restful and pleasant. She sat at one end of the bar. A middle-aged bartender smiled at her.

"Bourbon and water," she told him.

He brought the drink. The whiskey was better than average. She paid for it, and the price was no higher than at other places.

"This is a nice place," she told the bartender.

"We like to think it is," he nodded. "It's a fairly nice neighborhood—not too rich and not too poor. We get a good clientele."

"Career girls?"

"Quite a few. Secretaries, store buyers, advertising copywriters. The men run about the same. A few extras and others who work at the studios. Even a writer or two."

He left her to wait on a man who had come in and sat several stools away from her. He wore a sport jacket and slacks. He was very tan, and the brown skin contrasted sharply with his yellow hair.

Kima stared at her drink. The doctor had said it would be several days before he could be certain. Only he had sounded certain. Pregnant! Her hand tightened around her glass in reawakened fear.

What would she do? Where could she go?

"I'll get an abortion," she thought frantically. "There must be abortionists here. I've heard girls talk about them. I'll find one."

Then she remembered what some of the talk had been. The cost was high. Vaguely she remembered remarks about a thousand dollars—maybe more.

She drank some of her drink, knowing that she already was feeling the previous drinks. She put down the glass and looked at herself in the backbar mirror. She didn't like what she saw. She looked frightened. She looked tense and tired. She looked, she told herself, like an unmarried girl who finds herself pregnant.

"All right," she admonished herself. "Think calmly. You can go to Clint. Tell him. He's responsible—at least, as much as you are. It took both of you to do it! He has money—plenty of it. Maybe he can find the abortionist."

She finished the drink.

"No," she thought. "I can't go to Clint. I won't. I'm not certain that it *is*—I only *think* it is because we didn't use precautions. I won't go crying to him. I took my chances. It's my fault. Not his. I hate a crybaby."

The bartender stood in front of her again. He picked up her empty glass with a questioning expression.

"Another," she nodded. While he was getting it, she found a cigarette in her handbag. She couldn't find a match. The man in the sport jacket moved over and lit her cigarette for her.

"Thank you," Kima said. "That wasn't intentional."

"I didn't think so," he smiled. "You simply didn't have a match."

"I mean—"

"You aren't trying to pick me up. I know. But now that I'm here, may I stay to chat a while?"

She looked at him solemnly, very conscious of her drinks. Was this man trying to pick her up? And how had their conversation become so involved with pick-ups and intentions?

"May I stay?" he repeated.

"Certainly," she said. "As long as you understand."

"I understand."

The bartender brought Kima's drink. The man made no effort to pay for it when Kima firmly put her money on the bar.

When the bartender left, the man said, "My name is Tommy Suff. I play a little piano here and there. Been around a long time. Haven't I seen your picture lately?"

"Probably," Kima said bitterly. "If you read the scandal magazines. Does Kima Shannon mean anything to you?"

He nodded. "Rome. You and that Italian couple. Crazy!"

"Real crazy. No truth."

"Like you were framed?"

"Do you want to hear about it?" she asked. The drinks were fully in command now. She felt warm and friendly and at ease.

She didn't have a worry in the world. He was a nice young man who was interested, so she'd tell him the story.

He continued to nod and say, "Crazy, baby ... crazy ..." He bought her the next drink and four after that. When she had to go to the powder room she was unsteady. She splashed cold water into her face and took long, deep gulps of air, trying to sober herself. It didn't help much. She made up her face again and returned to the bar. Suff waited there for her.

"Look, baby, let's cut out of here," he said. "We'll eat. I know a place. We can dig some jazz later."

"Don't get ideas."

"I won't, baby."

When they left the soft light of the bar for the daylight that remained outside, Kima saw that Tommy Suff was older than she had thought. He probably was well toward his forties and he wore the lines of late hours and dissipation beneath the tan of his face.

He had a dilapidated convertible of uncertain vintage. They ate at a nondescript place where the food was better than she had anticipated when they went in. They had more drinks, and she felt warm and good about Tommy Suff. She didn't have to think, nor worry, nor face tomorrow or the next day. All that she wanted was escape, and the drinks and Tommy Suff gave her that.

The late afternoon and evening dissolved into night. They got in and out of the old convertible, they parked in lots, went into places, came out and went on.

In Hollywood they stopped at the Mann Hole.

"Jazz—crazy jazz, baby," Suff explained to her as they walked an unsteady route from the parked car to the place. "Shelly Mann's drums."

They went in and the music was there: pulsing, beating and exciting. They listened with others and Kima began to feel the contagious tempo of Tommy Suff's world.

"Like this was once for the beatniks," he told her, talking close into her ear above the music. "Now it's for the beat. Like Mike D. the columnist says. You dig Mike? The greatest. Come on, baby. Meet Dicky-boy and Shino and Flip and Honey-Lou."

She met Tommy Suff's friends; the musicians and the singers. They mingled and talked and she heard strange phrases.

"I need a fix," the small, dark man named Flip told Suff. "You got a connection, Tommy-boy? I can't make mine."

Suff shook his head and the small, dark man drifted away. The girl called Honey-Lou put her hand on Tommy's thigh. "Stud," she giggled.

"Baby, you're getting like smashed," he grinned. "Have you met my baby Kima?"

Honey-Lou smiled at Kima and turned her attention to a tall, dark young man who paused at the table and smiled down at her.

"*Listen*, Kima baby!" Tommy said. "Listen to that horn!"

They went on to other places. They drank. They found music, excitement and always a fresh drink. Everywhere Tommy Suff knew someone. Out on the beach at the Insomniac they listened to a woodwind jazz combo, and when they came out of the place—unsteady from the drinks, the music, the people and the places—he kissed her when they got into the car.

"Crazy, baby," he said. "Real crazy, Kima baby!"

They parked on Ventura in Studio City, and he took her into a place where the young men looked at her with hostility. The juke box played loudly and the boys shrieked gaily.

"Be a moment," Tommy mumbled. He left her by the door. She shut her eyes and leaned back against a wall and tried not to think of the femininely hateful looks being directed toward her by the feminine-acting males. Tommy talked earnestly with one of them across the room. After a few moments he rejoined Kima.

"He owed me loot," Tommy muttered. "Got it."

"I still have some," Kima murmured. She opened her pocketbook and took out several dollar bills and pressed them into his hand. "Take them, Tommy. Take them …"

"Baby, there's a party at a pad up Laurel Canyon. Come on."

She didn't remember the drive to the house. She must have dozed. When she opened her eyes it was difficult to focus them. The car radio was loudly blaring jazz into the night.

The house was not too large, nor too well furnished. A phonograph beat out progressive jazz. There weren't many lights. There were too many people and there was no organization of activities. They drank, they danced, they argued, and shrieked, and made love, and some of them wept.

A young man with a red beard swept Kima into his arms and kissed her wetly on the mouth.

Tommy wavered on to a group that greeted him noisily. The young man with the red beard said to Kima, "Come out and see the mountainside. Come out and see life. Come out where the air is fresh. The bomb has not come, and life must be lived."

Kima tried to stifle a giggle. "You're smashed," she said. That was what someone had said to a girl—Tommy had said it to Honey-Lou a long, long time ago in another place.

The young man led her outside. He was a large man, broad of shoulders, strong of torso. He wore a T-shirt and blue jeans. He took her down the road to where cars were parked and opened the door to the back seat of a sedan.

They sat side by side on the seat. He closed the door and locked it, and rolled up the windows.

Kima could smell the woods of the mountainside, and she heard crickets, and down the road the noises of the party.

"I'm Angelo, the last of the beats," the young man said. "The era is gone. The beat is gone. Now the students impress themselves with inadequate imitations. The true beats are dying, are dying. The beats are gone. I drink to drunkenness in sorrow."

"Let's go back to the party," Kima said, and shut her eyes. She was dizzy, drowsy and relaxed and she really didn't care what she did.

The young man forced her back on the car seat and bent over her.

"Now we'll make it together," he said. "This is the way it is for us. Far-out and beat for us."

His hands became busy with her and she shook her head from side to side and murmured, "No … no … no …"

"For the generation is beat," the young man said. "So beat. So ready. So dark. We'll make it together. You're soft and warm—round and full and made for love."

"No … no … no …" She tried to raise a hand, but it was too much effort. The world was whirling in a great swinging arc that became smaller and faster, tighter and concentric until she was clutching at him to keep from falling off into space.

This wasn't the way it should be. The outward pressure on her knees and the sound of slightly ripping underclothing. She knew what he was going to do, and she should stop him, only she was whirling too fast, and she was dizzy, so it was no use. It was easier to hang on to him. It was better, too.

Better now, and good, and she liked him because he was doing to her what a man could do. She kissed him and turned her head back and forth and said, "No! No! No!" even as she clung to him desperately and joined him in his frenzied, desperate exertions. She gasped and bit savagely at his lip. His hands were brutal upon her as they strained. Then they collapsed and were quiet, breathing hard.

After a while she opened her eyes and shoved him away. He moved readily and without protest. She got out of the car and rearranged her clothing. Suddenly she hated herself.

The man got out of the car.

"Ah, chick … you make it, and you make it. Far-out and sweet like female taking male," he mumbled in his drunken monotone.

"Get away from me," Kima said harshly. She slapped him with all her strength and ran back toward the house. She heard no footsteps behind her. When she looked back she saw the young, husky man leaning back against the car lighting a cigarette. He seemed indifferent to her actions.

She slowed and before she came to the house and the noise of the party she saw a high clump of brush. She almost staggered behind it because she was so suddenly nauseated. She vomited until she felt that she would fall. Her hands clutched at the brush for support and after a while she felt better.

Back in the house she found Tommy Suff.

"Where you been, baby?" he grinned. He was with a man and a girl who were violently arguing about something.

"Can we go home now, Tommy?"

"Sure, baby. Now."

He took her to the battered car and they drove back toward Hollywood. He didn't asked her where she lived, and she sat with closed eyes, trying to stay awake. Consciousness seemed to fade and return and fade again.

"Rocky?" he asked.

"Awful, Tommy."

He reached into the glove compartment and brought out a bottle. "Drink," he said. "It's brandy. It'll help."

"No. I'm sick."

"Drink it, baby. It really will help."

She lifted the bottle, took off the cap and drank. The brandy taste was not unpleasant. She drank again. Maybe it would make her feel well. Tommy took the bottle from her and returned it to the glove compartment.

"Go to sleep, Kima baby," he said. "I'll take care of you."

Obediently she shut her eyes, moving close to him and resting her head on his shoulder.

Much later she opened her eyes. She was on a bed, but there was no light pattern from the street upon the ceiling. Confused, she looked around in the half-dark and saw a strange room.

Someone was beside her. As if she had been burned, she turned and saw Tommy Suff's head on the pillow. She glanced down his length of body. He was without clothing, and her own clothing was draped over a chair. Her movement awakened Suff.

"You're wonderful, baby," he whispered. He reached for her and pulled her down on the bed beside him.

"Tommy ... no ... please ..." she said, trying to squirm away from him.

He laughed softly and rolled his weight upon her.

"Baby ... baby ..." he said. "Pretty baby." He kissed her and held her beneath him. She was too weak to prevent him from taking her again—she was certain it was again, although she couldn't remember the first time.

Once his lips touched her cheeks and he whispered, "Don't cry, Kima baby. Why tears?" But he didn't stop his rhythmic exertions and Kima bit her lips and tried not to sob out loud. She had only herself to blame, she thought.

She turned her head and stared at the window. The blind was drawn, but she saw the first gray of dawn against it.

Tommy was holding her tightly now, whispering the uninhibited love words that some men find when they near fulfillment with a woman.

"Baby ... baby ... baby ..." he gasped and strained her against him.

She felt nothing—only the wetness upon her cheeks and the pain of her lip where she bit it.

CHAPTER THIRTEEN

TOMMY SUFF LIVED in a run-down court apartment in an older part of Venice. At midmorning he made coffee for them after his tentative suggestion that they make love again had been refused.

"I can't blame you," he said huskily. "Hangover. Maybe I've got a drink somewhere. I think I brought in the brandy."

The thought sickened Kima. She had dressed and used the bathroom. Seldom in her life had she felt so desolate, ill and hopeless as she did at this moment. In the morning light, after the long night of dissipation, Tommy Suff looked wan and dissolute. The small apartment needed cleaning. Dirty dishes were in the sink.

"I have to go home," Kima said.

"I'll drive you after we have some coffee. Where do you live?"

"In an old part of Hollywood."

"Okay. I got to see a guy there, anyhow."

He left her suddenly and went to the bathroom. She could hear him being sick. He returned looking pale.

"These goddamn hangovers—they kill me, baby."

The coffee was perking. He poured two cups and laced them strongly with brandy.

Kima shuddered. "I couldn't, Tommy—not with the brandy."

"Try it. Just try it. I mean like it will help, baby."

He sounded so serious and friendly about it that she did try a few sips. At first she disliked the taste, but she forced herself to drink the cup of liquid and she began to feel better. The hot coffee and brandy apparently did help.

Finally they were ready to leave. They went out to the convertible and he drove toward Hollywood.

"Kima baby, you're like crazy in bed. You know that? When do we make it again?"

"I don't know, Tommy." She didn't dare look at him. She would be ill if she did. She hated him, but she hated herself even more for the night and what had happened. She couldn't really blame him. He was a man. He had a right to expect it of her after what had happened.

He tried to make conversation, but she answered in monosyllables and eventually he became silent. He let her out at her apartment building.

"Hey, baby—you forgot to give me your phone number. I'll call you later."

"I won't be home, Tommy. I'm—I mean, I'm leaving town."

Anything to end it, to close off this sordid chapter of her life. She quickly crossed the sidewalk and went into the building. Behind her she heard Tommy's car take off with a grinding of gears, as if he might be suddenly angry.

Her telephone was ringing as she put her key in the lock. She hurried to get inside and across the room to the telephone. She answered it and a man's voice said, "Kima?"

"Yes. Who is this?"

"You don't know me. I'm Hi Dayton—photographer. I need a model for some stills. A friend of yours—Carla Flaxon—called me yesterday and said you might be available."

"Carla Flaxon?"

"Yes. She said you've been having some bad luck. I know what she means, Kima. I saw the pictures. But it won't make any difference for these particular pictures. Of course, it's just model work, but Carla said you might need some extra work right now."

"I don't get it," Kima said suspiciously. "Carla and I—"

The man seemed to be indifferent. "I don't know about any of that. I just know I've known Carla a long time and she knows I need models. She said if you ask why she recommended you, to tell you to forget what happened—that she'll call you soon."

"I still don't understand."

"Look, Kima—Miss Shannon—you want this job or not? I pay going rates. Make up your mind."

"I'll take it," Kima said doubtfully. She needed every cent she could earn. Maybe she had misjudged Carla. Sometimes a girl who had come up through the seamier side of life could be the best friend in an emergency. "Where's your studio?"

He told her and set a date for two hours from then.

When she finished talking with him, Kima dialed Bill Rold's office again. Again he was out of the office. She hung up and got ready for her date at the photographic studio.

She assumed the work was for fashion pictures. There was a heavy business in that type of modeling as the women's wear manufacturers continued to expand and build their business on the West Coast. Thousands of pictures were used every year for advertising, catalogues, brochures and the multitude of promotions constantly emanating from the fashion world.

Before leaving for Rome, she had sold the Volkswagen for a few hundred dollars, vaguely intending to buy a car when she got to Europe. After her return she had no money to buy one.

Getting around by bus and taxi was slow and inconvenient, but it was better than trying to rent or buy a car right now. The photographic studio was in the Hollywood area. She took a taxi to the old building that housed it and went up to the floor where it was listed in a creaking old elevator.

A prematurely bald young man with a dark, swarthy skin was working at a desk in a small receptionist's office when she came in. He looked up at her.

"Kima Shannon?" he asked.

"Yes."

"I'm Hi Dayton. I'm working alone today. Be with you in a moment."

He motioned her to a chair where she waited until he finished typing a letter on an old typewriter. He put the letter in an envelope.

"Okay, Kima, let's get on with it. Come on back to the studio."

The main studio room was barren and shabby. Several background flats were stacked against a wall. Lighting equipment looked battered and old. A daybed with garish pillows was shoved against one wall. A tall screen concealed one corner of the studio.

Dayton tossed her a filmy, black, short nightgown. "Start with this," he said.

She felt and saw the transparency of the gown, and glanced apprehensively at Dayton.

"Are these lingerie shots?" she asked.

"Yeah," he grunted. He was busy arranging light stands by the daybed. A camera already was positioned there.

"Nothing under?" she asked quietly.

"Don't worry. I'll use lighting to conceal enough. Come on, baby—I got to work against time at the rate I pay you chicks."

Still apprehensive, but slightly reassured by his complaint about fees and time, she retired behind the screen and undressed to put on the nightgown. There was a simple cotton wrapper draped over a chair and she threw it around herself. The nightgown was very short and very low.

Dayton hardly glanced at her when she came out. He was fussing with a spotlight and swearing steadily under his breath. "On the daybed," he said over his shoulder.

Not knowing exactly what he wanted of her, she went to the daybed and sat there waiting for his direction. Finally he had the spotlight working to his satisfaction. He turned on other lights so that Kima was almost blinded by the glare.

"A seduction pose, baby," Dayton said.

"What do you mean?"

He came to the daybed and without hesitation raised her legs and twisted her body around so that she was stretched out on the bed. The nightgown slipped almost up to her waist and he nonchalantly looked down at her and smiled.

"Real nice stuff, Kima," he said. He contemplated her with narrowed eyes. "On second thought, why the nightgown? You're a cinch for the girlie mags with knockers like those."

Unceremoniously he reached down and deftly pulled the nightgown up and over her head. His hands cupped her breasts and squeezed, pinching the nipples with his fingers. "They like 'em hard and ready," he grinned lasciviously.

The sudden shock of his actions and the realization of what he was doing froze Kima into motionless acceptance before her anger could break through.

When it did, she slapped blindly at his face. He cursed and stepped back. "What was that for?" he demanded.

"What do you think I am?" she cried. "What kind of pictures are these supposed to be?"

"What the hell kind do you think they are?" he retorted. "Nudes, baby. Maybe some under-the-counter stuff. You want to work in a few stag movies and I'll fix that for you, too. So don't pull this innocent crap with me. Carla said you're hep."

"She said I'd pose for pornography?" Kima stared at him in disbelief.

"Knock it off, honey. So you've made your little production scene. You want me to believe you never did it before—so okay. I believe you. Only I saw them Italian shots. Real good, too. Them *paparazzi* got a good thing going for them. But that's in Rome—and we're here. So why don't you just lay back and let me get a few shots of that well-stacked stuff you got?"

Kima sprang from the daybed, clutching the flimsy night-gown to her for what concealment it gave. She ran across the room and frantically started to dress.

Hi Dayton followed her. "Hey! What gives? Carla says you even done some hustling now and then. So why the big thing about posing for a few shots?"

"Carla is a damned liar!" Kima shrieked at him. She jammed a zipper in her angry hurry. "A damned liar! Let me out of here. Just let me out. That's all I want."

"Okay! Okay!"

Kima slammed the door after her, and tried to keep tears of anger out of her eyes. She passed the elevator and went down the stairs, stopping on a landing to dry her eyes and apply fresh lipstick.

Carla deliberately had entrapped her, viciously putting her in a nauseating situation, and was probably laughing about it. Furthermore, she probably would broadcast that Kima Shannon was posing for girlie pictures, booking herself for pornography bits. Carla had that kind of a dangerous tongue.

Kima left the old office building and walked. Her fury began to die and she thought of the night before and what had happened: the young, large man with the red beard, and Tommy Suff in his shabby apartment. Just how low *was* she?

Few tramps would be more promiscuous than she had been on the previous night. No smart girl would have allowed herself to drink enough to get in a situation like that; or, for that matter, in the situation in Rome. Maybe Hi Dayton had every reason to believe that she would pose for his nude pictures, or even his stag movies.

And what of Bill Rold? He had left money for her that night after he had slept with her. True—he had called immediately afterward and assured her that it was a loan. But did he really think that?

Above and beyond all that, she was pregnant. An unmarried, pregnant woman.

She had to stop this insane downward ride she was taking. Most of all she needed a job—a decent job before she became ensnared in more degradations such as she had experienced in the last twenty-four hours.

She would see Bill Rold again and ask his aid. Impress upon him how important it was for her to find work.

His office was within a short taxi ride and she went there at once. The receptionist recognized her and called on the intercom.

"He'll see you," she smiled.

Bill Rold greeted her in his office. "I know, darling—you called. But I've been out quite a bit."

"Bill, I really need that job. Desperately."

"I've tried to find something for you, Kima. But I simply haven't had any luck. If you need money to tide you over—"

"No. I didn't come here for that. I still have the—the *loan* you left." She gazed at him and saw the nervous flick of his eyes away from her. "Bill—*was* that a loan?"

He met her eyes instantly. "Now wait a second, baby—don't think that I—"

"I don't know *what* to think now!" she interrupted. "I did think there was something there for us. More than just a man and a woman getting into bed together. Or am I being too blunt?"

"Okay," he said. "Let's bring it out in the open. Maybe there was something. I did feel something extra. It was beginning to build. It started that night in Vegas. And maybe it could have become something big."

"But not now?" she asked quietly.

His eyes steadily held hers. "No. Not now. I'll go all out for you—in a way. You need help? You can have it. I'll give you money, and no strings. But it can't be anything else—nothing big for us."

"Not even big enough for you to recommend me to some of your business friends? Are you afraid I'd want to lay them?"

"Stop talking like a tramp."

"Why should I? You think I am. You don't say it, but you think it. Did I go to bed too easily with you, Bill? Is that it? Was I too much of a pushover? An easy roll in the hay?"

"All right. You asked. I'll answer. *Were you?* I only know what happened. You and Nytrack in Vegas. That stuff from Rome. A few drinks with me and we're in bed. *You* answer, Kima. I'd like to know!"

"Oh, God—and I might have fallen in love with you," she whispered.

Abruptly she turned and left the office, running down a short hallway, past the startled office workers and receptionist, and out into the main hallway. She hurried to the elevator. As its door opened she heard Bill Rold behind her, calling, "Kima—wait. Wait—"

"Go to hell," she said.

She stepped into the elevator. The girl operator looked at her with raised eyebrows, but didn't comment. Kima was thankful that they stopped for no other passengers on the way down.

A taxi took her back to the apartment. She bathed and changed clothes. Afterward she ate alone and went to a movie. She hardly knew what she saw, but by the time she left the theater and returned home her thoughts were clearer than they had been for several days.

She prepared for bed and took two aspirins, scorning the temptation of a strong drink of bourbon. She was dead tired and she slept soundly all night.

For two days she answered ads, visited employment agencies and tried in every way that she could to find a job. There were two or three vague promises—"Call back next week" ... "Leave us your number—we may have a vacancy soon"—but she found no job.

On the morning of the third day, the nagging worry uppermost in her mind sent her to the telephone as soon as she thought that the doctor might be in his office.

The doctor was out on calls. He would be in shortly after noon.

Kima set out upon her round of job-hunting again. It was a fruitless hunt. At two o'clock she called the doctor from a pay booth.

"This is Mrs. Kay Shannon, Doctor. You said you'd have the laboratory report today—"

"Oh, yes. I just looked at it, and you and your husband should be very happy, Mrs. Shannon! You're undoubtedly pregnant. I'd suggest that you come in tomorrow or the next day and we'll—"

Holding her breath with sudden fear, Kima carefully replaced the telephone on its hook. For a few moments she stood silently in the booth and impulsively pressed her hands low against her body. There was a child there now, a living child. From some vaguely remembered source she thought: *I am with child ... I am with child ... I am with child....*

She left the booth and went directly to the small apartment. This time she did not ignore the bottle of bourbon. She needed the drink. She felt weak.

One stiff portion was enough for the time. She gagged a little getting it down. She replaced the bottle and rinsed the glass. She went to a window and looked down into the street. She had to think what to do. Everything was becoming centered in vital realities now.

The telephone rang. Kima answered it and Milo Ginz said, "Kima, darling. You got a job yet?"

"No, Milo—do you have something?" Her hopes took a leap upward.

"No, but I got other news for you. Ironical, like they say in novels. From Rome I got friends who say the rushes on you—the takes before he sent you home—were terrific. Even Nytrack says so! Even if he isn't using them. But word's around. You're terrific. No one will touch you now, but later you maybe got it made."

"So?"

"So? Ach, Kima—don't sound so low, yes? Please, for me? In a while—a year maybe—things will be different. People forget. You need money?"

"No, Milo, Look—can I call you back tomorrow or the next day. Maybe we can talk then?"

"Something is wrong, Kima? I mean worse than—?"

"No ... no, Milo. I just have to think something out. When I do, then I'll call you."

"Okay then, darling. You call."

"And thanks for telling me about the film—the rushes. It's nice to know that you're a successful failure."

It took two hours before she got a call through to Clint.

"Hiyah, Kima, baby!" he yelped when she identified herself. "You sure been raising hell for yourself!" He laughed and she knew that he had been drinking. But somehow his voice was reassuring. She realized that they had been together for many hours in the past. Now she hated what she was about to do to him, but there was no other way; no other place to go. At least, not yet ...

"Clint, I've got to see you," she said.

"You sound very serious, baby. Something wrong?"

"Very much. Can I see you tonight?"

"Well, I sort of have a date with Carla."

"Clint, this is terribly important. *Please?*"

"Can't you tell me now?"

"No. I have to talk with you. I need your advice and some help. I want to *talk* with you—*be* with you—Clint."

Evidently the seriousness of her voice impressed him.

He said, "Where are you living? I'll pick you up. Right away. Carla's still at the studio. I'll have someone call her and tell her I'm tied up in conference."

She gave him the address and while she waited for him she tried to think out what she would say to him.

For some strange reason she was surprised that he had not changed in the weeks since they had seen one another. He still was the dark-haired, fresh-looking, young and lean man that she remembered from their first meeting. He grinned and kissed her heartily.

"Baby!" he said. "It's good to see you. And don't tell me—that Italian jazz about you. Crap. Pure crap!"

"Oh, Clint—I'm so damned glad to see you!"

"I'm hungry and I know a place. We'll have some drinks and save your problems until then. Okay?"

"A place where Carla won't come?" she asked.

He laughed. "You think of everything. She won't be there. And what's this somber and serious bit you gave me over the phone?"

"Let's—let's wait until dinner."

He selected a small and cozy place in Beverly Hills. He insisted that they have several drinks before they ordered, and she was glad to have them. She hated the task before her.

They ate and he told her about what was happening at PAK and on his series.

"TV sure is taking over the town," he smiled. "The big picture producers are running scared. Like to Italy and France and England. And, baby—I hear the rushes on you in Nytrack's picture were really terrific!"

"I know." She fingered the glass holding the after-dinner drink he had ordered. "Clint—I've got to talk with you now. I don't want to, but I don't know what else to do."

"Talk, baby. And remember—think positive?" he grinned.

"Clint …" She reached across the small table and put a hand on one of his. Suddenly she was frightened. What did men do when girls told them what she was about to say? "Clint …"

He smiled at her and waited.

"Clint, I'm pregnant. It's yours."

His smile became oddly frozen upon his lips. Then his eyes narrowed, and his voice became sober.

"Hey now, baby," he said. "Not that jazz …"

She recoiled as if he had slapped her. "Clint—I'm not trying to—"

Abruptly the harshness faded out of his eyes and an expression of surprise came into them.

"Goddamn!" he exclaimed. "That night. I remember. You asked me to use something and I didn't. Jesus! Maybe you're right!"

"I'm not asking you to marry me. I'm—Clint, I don't know what to *do*."

"Hell, that's easy. I know a doctor—it'll cost a grand, but I got nothing but dough. We'll take care of it."

"I hadn't thought about that—I mean, I don't know if—"

"Christ! You don't *want* the kid, do you?" he grinned. "I'm sorry it happened, and I guess I'm to blame. I believe you about that. But there's only one way out. I'll fix it up for you and pay for it." He laughed. "Carla would murder me if she knew!"

"Please, Clint," Kima said. She didn't want him to act this way, as if it were a joke. A baby wasn't a joke. And the thought of an abortion sent a chill through her. She'd like to tell him what Carla had done to her, too. But she knew it would not be wise. Things between Carla and Clint were too solid.

He saw the distress in her eyes and stopped smiling. He was just an overgrown boy; an adult who lacked maturity; a good-looking young man who had played a role so long in a TV series that he approached the realities of life with a quip and a character rendition.

"I'm sorry," he said. "But it's happened. We've got an out. And the best thing we can do right now is to have some more drinks and give ourselves hell for being so careless."

They stared at one another across the table, and Kima smiled thinly. Maybe he was right. He didn't want the child. He certainly didn't want her. But he was willing to get her out of her trouble;

to pay for it. Whatever prompted him, some measure of decency made him accept partial responsibility. The method might be wrong, but at least he was not turning his back upon her.

"All right," she said. "Order the drinks. We'll drink to that—whatever it is."

He ordered for them and they sat there for two hours drinking steadily, talking softly, not making much sense as time went on, and even becoming sentimental toward the end.

"Gotta go," Clint suddenly announced. "Gotta go now. Show you my new place up in the hills."

They left and he drove her in a new Thunderbird through traffic to winding, climbing streets that were almost elaborate lanes that meandered among carefully separated homes.

He turned into a driveway and carelessly parked in front of a new house. It looked low, sprawling and expensive.

He took her inside and showed her a large living room, the swimming pool at the side of the house, the rooms and hallways and the luxuries.

When they came to the master bedroom he looked at her and they both laughed a little in their intoxication.

"What's the difference now?" he grinned. "I mean, baby we started it. And we had something then—like it was—and maybe before we finish it…?"

"I've drunk too much. Much too much," she said. "It's getting to be a habit."

He put his hands on her arms and shook his head. "I got that urge to make it with you again. Not permanent like, but you know?"

"I know," Kima said.

He led her to the bed and they stretched out on it. She was confused by an onslaught of strange emotions. This was the man who had impregnated her, the man who had made love to her.

Nor was he denying his responsibility, nor turning away from her. She felt a deep, warm gratitude toward him; and a return of excitement in just the knowledge that he had made her pregnant.

When he kissed her she automatically responded to him. Perhaps of all the men who had taken her in the last few weeks, he had a greater right than any. At least he was not deserting her when she needed him—not as Ken Nytrack had done, as Bill Rold had done.

"Oh, Clint," she suddenly sobbed and turned to him and held on to him tightly as she let tears come. "Clint … Clint … Clint …"

"It's all right, baby. Relax. I'll take care of everything. Just relax, baby." He began to stroke her soothingly. She gradually unwound under his hands. The tension, worry and fear began to disappear. The many drinks had brought the familiar drowsiness and letdown of inhibitions. When his fingers sought the fastening to her clothing, she helped him, and was glad to feel his embrace.

In a strange fantasy it seemed to her as if this were almost a marriage bed. Certainly their intimacy was natural. It once had conceived a child.

She helped him disrobe her and he was with her, holding her, whispering to her. He had drunk much and his voice was thick now, but she barely recognized the thickness as she surrendered to her own drowsy intoxication and receptiveness to love-making.

The full glare of overhead lights was almost like a flash of lightning. Kima struggled to sit up and Clint swore under his breath. They both looked toward the door, where Carla Flaxon stood, hands on hips, her eyes alive with fury.

"You bitch!" she said softly as she advanced into the room. "You two-bit tramp. Get off that bed!"

"Now, Carla—" Clint protested in his thick voice. He sat on the edge of the bed and stared at the advancing blonde. Kima got off the bed and faced the actress, feeling completely defenseless in her nudity.

"Carla!" Clint said again.

Carla sprang at Kima, her fingers curved into claws as she slashed at Kima's face and breasts. Kima fell back upon the bed and the blonde fell upon her.

The two women fought without words, gasping, scratching, biting. Clint got away from the bed and absentmindedly stepped into trousers. He watched the women with a surprised and almost sardonic smile.

"Like crazy!" he said. "My God, two dames—they fight like crazy! Like cats!"

Carla sank her fingers into Kima's black hair and jerked hard. Kima screamed with pain. The blonde pulled Kima off the bed to the floor. In a scrambling, fighting rage they moved across the floor, Carla dragging Kima by the hair as Kima desperately tried to get to her feet.

At the doorway she scraped the side of her nude body against a door jamb and felt the pain. They swayed and struggled along a hallway to the living room, across it and to the entrance door.

Somehow Carla managed to get the door open. She shoved Kima out and slammed the door behind her.

Kima leaned against the side of the house, trying to get her breath, shivering in the coolness of the night. Inside the house Carla was screaming at Clint.

Kima turned and ran. She had to get away from this house. She didn't know where she could go, and she had no clothing, but she had to get away. The fight had left her panic-stricken. She had to hide.

Grass was coldly wet upon her bare feet. She crossed the yard of another home. Somewhere behind her Clint called, but she didn't stop. She would come back later ... later.

She was on an asphalt roadway between hedges. Her throat and lungs hurt from gasping for air. She was intoxicated and sick and hurt. She had to keep on running. She had to run and hide—

A car stopped and hands seized her. She shut her eyes and struggled until one of the hands slapped her smartly across a cheek. The slap stopped her hysteria. She opened her eyes and saw the uniform of a policeman. A police car was parked at the side of the roadway. Another policeman was watching. After a moment he went to the car and returned with a blanket. He draped it over Kima's naked body.

"All right," the cop who held her said. "Now we'd better go in and find out what this is all about."

"You can't!" Kima cried. "You mustn't!"

"She's really stoned!" the second patrolman murmured. "Some of these babes sure drink it up."

"And live it up!" the other cop smirked. "Okay, lady—into the car."

They released her the following morning, but not before a news reporter got the essentials of the story. He called his city desk and they sent a photographer to get a shot of her as she was released. She had been allowed a call—and she sobbed over the telephone to Milo. He came at once, paid a fine for her and got her released. He also brought some clothing for her.

The reporter was insistent.

"But where *were* you?" he asked. "Who was throwing the party?"

"Please leave me alone," Kima said.

That was his last attempt. Milo interceded and the reporter shrugged and turned away. He had a good story. Kima Shannon was getting to be headline material.

Milo took her home.

"You want to tell me?" he asked.

She shook her head.

"All right," Milo said gently. "You better get some sleep. Maybe you call me later?"

"Yes. And thanks, Milo."

He smiled and patted her hand. "You're my client, no? You got great possibilities. You're a good property, darling."

"I'm glad you think so," she told him with a rueful smile.

She fell into an exhausted sleep and was awakened early in the afternoon by the telephone. It was Clint.

"Baby, I owe you something real big," he said. "I saw the story in the paper. You didn't tell them where you were. And listen, baby—I'm real sorry. I mean about Carla and all that. I tried to find you."

"I know."

"But I fixed the other."

She was silent, thinking about what he had just said.

"You mean—the *other*?" she finally asked.

"It's all set. Tomorrow morning. I'm not working so I'll take you there. Ten o'clock. I even paid the dough."

"Clint—I'm not certain—"

"Don't worry about him, baby. He's good."

"But I—"

"Look, Kima—I got to hang up. Carla just drove into the driveway. I'll come by for you about nine in the morning. Don't worry."

The telephone clicked in her ear and the line went dead.

So it was fixed. Clint had made all the arrangements. Tonight she would be pregnant and in trouble. Tomorrow night she would no longer be pregnant. The small, new life that she sheltered in her body would be destroyed and gone.

Although she had no appetite, she opened some soup and made toast and coffee. She took a long, hot bath and went back to bed. She still felt exhausted from the ordeal she had been through. Almost immediately she was asleep.

CHAPTER FOURTEEN

C LINT was not in his usual gay mood. He looked serious and worried.

"This gets me," he told her. "I mean all that happened the night before last and that lousy story the next morning. You're getting all the bad breaks—and none of it really your fault."

"Some of it is," she said. "You know that as well as I do."

"I ought to slap Carla down," he said frankly. "Only—I got a hell of a thing about her, Kima. I can't help myself." He glanced at her. "I know she's a bitch in your book. She is in a lot of books. But she's got something."

"I think you almost enjoyed watching us fight that night."

"I don't know. I'm honest with you. I don't know. Maybe a man's got a lot of—well, something in him that makes him like a thing like that. Two women tangling."

"Why are you doing this for me today?" Kima asked. "Be honest about it, Clint. For a while last night I thought I knew. Maybe we had something. Now I'm not certain."

"You mean reasons like one, two, three, four?"

"I guess so."

"Easy. I like you. We made it together. We got caught. I've got plenty of dough and the right connections. And I still like you—remember that. So we take care of things. It's worse on you than it is on me. I'm sorry about that. But you don't have to worry about the money and that part of it."

"I *guess* I know what you mean."

"You sound scared."

"I am. I never was so scared in my life, Clint."

"You never had one of these before?"

"No."

"I've talked with girls who have—even paid for some. They say it really isn't so bad, Kima. Honest."

"I'm still scared."

"You're going through with it, aren't you?" He sounded suddenly alarmed.

"Yes."

He finally parked near an older office building.

"I won't go up with you," he said. "The studio called this morning. I got to go in for some retakes. But it's all set. Room 513. You go right in. The doc will be waiting. He's been paid. He'll want you to stay a while afterward. I'll give you an extra hundred for any medical stuff you may need—taxi home and stuff."

"Clint—can't you come with me?" she asked, suddenly on the verge of panic.

"Baby, I can't. I'm almost late now. Besides, the doc doesn't like to have the men around. He wants to handle things himself."

He gave her the extra money and opened the door for her. She didn't look back, but she heard the Thunderbird draw away from the curb and from the corner of her eye she saw it go past her. Clint was looking straight ahead. Kima went into the building.

The doctor had thinning gray hair. He wore a white smock, not unlike those worn by male beauty operators. He was smoking a cigarette and reading a magazine when Kima went into the office. He glanced up at her.

"What's your first name?" he asked.

"Kima."

He nodded. "Come into the other room."

She followed him into a small office furnished as a surgery. An antiquated operating table with metal stirrups was set up. The sheet on the table looked slightly soiled. An old sterilizing case similar to those used by dentists many years ago held some instruments. In one corner of the office was a large, white waste basket. Stains on it looked as if they had been made by blood.

"Get out of your clothes," the man said. He had a scrawny, unhealthy appearance. Two fingers on his right hand were heavily stained by cigarette smoke. "When you're undressed, get on the table."

Nonchalantly he went to a dirty washbasin and washed his hands. He dried them on a paper towel from a container above the basin.

Hesitantly Kima looked at the man. He seemed to be surprised and a little angry that she had not begun to undress.

"Are you an M.D.?" Kima asked bluntly.

"Don't worry about that. I've had good training. I've taken care of four or five thousand women this way."

"But that sheet looks dirty. And those instruments—don't they have to be sterilized? I mean…"

"I'll give you a shot of penicillin. That'll take care of things. Now hurry up."

She remained motionless, staring at him.

"Look, girlie—you'd better get out of those pants you're wearing if you want me to get you out of the trouble you got from taking them off for somebody else."

"I don't know—"

"You're a good-looking kid. You're paid for. But sometimes I can make it a lot easier if you want to be nice to me first," he grinned "How about it?"

She looked around the room again. She saw bloody gauze in the large white waste basket. She saw stains on the floor at the end of the table, where the stirrups obscenely awaited her.

She thought of undressing in front of this man, of getting on the table, of opening her body to him. She saw the instruments in the dirty glass case, and she thought about the cell of life she nurtured within her. She had come here to destroy it; to allow this uncouth, slightly dirty, lasciviously smiling man to kill that cell of life. This man who callously suggested intercourse before abortion. *I can make it a lot easier if you want to be nice to me first.*

"No," Kima said softly. She looked around the room again and back again into the man's face. "No!"

He tried to stop her, for some reason or other, and she shoved him so violently that he crashed against the small table holding the glass case of instruments. The case crashed to the floor, spewing its metal contents over the soiled, brown linoleum.

Kima ran from the office and down the five flights of stairs. She slowed to a fast walk on the street, afraid to look back for fear that the man with the gray hair would be there, yet knowing that he would never follow her.

She saw a sidewalk telephone booth and went into it and found a dime in her handbag. With trembling fingers she dialed the one number that she could remember. She sighed with relief when she heard Sam Berill's familiar voice.

"Sam, it's Kima. I have to see you. At once. I need you."

"Where are you?

She told him.

"Stay there," he said. "I'll be there in twenty minutes."

They were in his apartment. She finished telling him the complete story. Anxiously she looked into his face.

"And that's all of it," she said. "All of it, Sam. The story of a tramp, I guess."

"Don't say that! Don't ever say that!" he said angrily. He got up from his easy chair and crossed the room to the chair where she sat. He leaned down and kissed her on the forehead.

"I'm not even going to say, 'You poor kid,' " he told her. "It happened. It could happen to a hell of a lot of girls. This is Hollywood. Worse *has* happened. Worse probably will. Yours is rough enough, but you're alive and you have friends—and talent."

"So?"

"You wouldn't consider marrying me, would you, Kima?" he asked. "I'm halfway through my thirties, and a little shopworn. But I work hard, and I'll be nice to you."

"Would you be kind to my child?" she smiled, suddenly near tears.

"Need I answer? And you won't marry me?"

"No, Sam. I guess I don't love you that way. I love you this way—it's worse because I turn to you for help and offer you so very little in return."

"If Clinton weren't so damned big I might beat hell out of him."

"That isn't an answer. He thought he was doing the right thing. Besides, I'm as much to blame as he is."

"What do you really want to do, Kima?"

"Have the baby. But I don't know how to go about it—where to go. I thought maybe you could tell me what unmarried pregnant women do, Sam. You've been a newspaperman and things."

He looked at her thoughtfully. "Yeah ... I guess I know. And maybe we can work something out. And you're right. I *am* a newspaperman. Maybe that's why I haven't any good clients left here—none that pay me a living. So ..." He paused to light a cigarette.

"That gives you an idea?"

"Up in Oregon I have a good friend. I worked there for a few years. This friend is running a good, small newspaper and he wants me to take the city desk for him. I've even been thinking sort of seriously about it—especially when I haven't been able to pay the rent lately."

"Why don't you do it, Sam? I think you'd be happier. You're not—not cruel enough for this town."

"Let me finish," he grinned. "You say you have a little money, and I could help." He held up a protesting hand as she started to interrupt. "Make it a loan, then ... we'll figure that out later. But you could be a young widow—or a divorcee. It's a nice, medium-size town. There are several small hospitals and convalescent homes around. I think my pal might even arrange a job of some sort for you. We're sort of real close friends."

Kima looked into his slightly battered face and saw the strength in it that sometimes she forgot to see. She realized how right she had been about him. He was strong, but he was not cruel enough to exist in his chosen profession in this town of unrealities and exaggerations.

She said, "I still have to straighten things out somehow with Clint. There'll be nothing between us ever again, and I guess it really will be no different in a way from if I had married him and was divorced."

"He could have married you," Sam said curtly. "Back then."

"He's going to marry Carla."

Sam looked away from her for a moment. He put out his cigarette and took a deep breath.

"You haven't heard the news?" he said.

"What do you mean?"

"Clint and Carla were married last week in Vegas. They've kept it under wraps because of a non-marriage clause in her contract. But a stringer for a San Francisco paper caught up with it. It hit the radio and TV newscasts late this morning. While you were at the quack's place, I guess."

Kima stared at him. "Then I guess that's that," she finally said. She smiled and shook her head. "Sam, are you being honest about wanting to leave here and go to Oregon to work on that paper?"

"If I hadn't been worrying about you, I'd have gone two weeks ago. I couldn't stop hoping—about us, I mean. I'll call him right now. And—no strings. Okay?"

"It has to be that way. Only a heart loaded with gratitude, Sam. And maybe in—seven and a half months, I guess—well, maybe things will be all changed again."

"Will you ever want to come back, Kima?"

She didn't answer at once, but thoughtfully stood and went to a window and looked out upon a limited view of Hollywood. When she turned back to Sam she was smiling wryly.

"Sam, listen to me. They say I have talent. I understand they were excited about me when they saw the rushes in Rome. Milo says in a year or so people will have forgotten. Others have come back—greater stars than I may ever be—after things just as bad or worse."

Sam nodded silently.

"Yes," she said. "I'll come back. Somehow—sometime. But I'll go to Oregon with you, Sam. No strings. Just us and this baby I'm going to have. For whatever may work out for all of us—each of us—together or apart."

"That's good enough for me," Sam said. He came across the room and kissed her, on the lips, almost reverently.

She smiled up at him and nodded.

He left her and went to the telephone and grinning broadly he dialed.

"Operator," he said. "I want to place a call to Oregon."

THE END